A Song Amongst the Orange Trees

Sara Alexi is the author of the Greek Village Series.
She divides her time between England and a small village
in Greece.

http://facebook.com/authorsaraalexi

Sara Alexi

A SONG AMONGST THE ORANGE TREES

A Novella

oneiro

Published by Oneiro Press 2015

ISBN-10: 1515168069
ISBN-13: 978-1515168065

Also by Sara Alexi

The Illegal Gardener
Black Butterflies
The Explosive Nature of Friendship
The Gypsy's Dream
The Art of Becoming Homeless
In the Shade of the Monkey Puzzle Tree
A Handful of Pebbles
The Unquiet Mind
Watching the Wind Blow
The Reluctant Baker
The English Lesson
The Priest's Well

Dedicated, with thanks, to Emrys Plant for his beautiful poem that by the wonder of story telling became the lyrics to a song.

Kharkiv, the Ukraine

The light is utterly blinding. The sun is piercing straight through Sakis' eyelids and boring deep into his throbbing head. The ringing in his left ear, long and high-pitched, is relentless, an internal sound that does not diminish as he turns his head to press the noise into the pillow. His heart is pulsating in his neck, thumping at his temple and pounding deep inside his brain. Summersaulting up from his guts, a bubble rises and pushes through his chest until it reaches his lips. His happiness bursts as a grin, extinguishing all physical pain, cutting through his hangover, conquering his tinnitus. He won!

A noise, china clinking. Cup upon saucer? The door to the bedroom is not altogether closed. There is someone in the sitting area. Should he be alarmed?

Trying to sit up generates resistance. His stomach complains and strongly suggests relieving his body of its contents. His head, meanwhile, assures him that if he moves from horizontal, it will drop from his shoulders like a lead shot and grind a rolling course across the floor. Lying very still is the only immediate option. Lying absolutely still, staring at the hotel ceiling with a big grin on his face.

How quickly life changes. He performed without expectation. It could have been his chance but, at the time, he felt without doubt that it was the wrong song. It was too light, ephemeral, with so little meaning, and definitely not his best. He told them at the committee meeting that it was too obvious, that it held no history, no gravitas. Stepping from the stage, despite the thunderous applause, he was certain it was over. He slunk, head down, back into the semi-circular seating booth. Andreas shouted a customary 'Bravo' above the noise of the crowd and threw a big arm around his shoulder and pulled him in for a hug, a big smile puckering his chubby cheeks, his eyes bright. The applause didn't stop and an unusual feeling of static began to electrify the air around them. A stranger bounded up, kissed him on both cheeks, and talked earnestly to his manager, who then released him from his embrace. From somewhere, a glass of champagne was slipped into his hand, a television camera was pushed in his face, and a girl with a Scandinavian accent began to ask him questions, her bubbly concentration fully focused on him until the scores began to roll in. A Greek official squeezed into the booth with them. He shouted over the noise of twenty thousand spectators that the big man he had brought with him would be Sakis' new bouncer. It seemed his oversized manager was suddenly not enough.

Then people he did not know squeezed into the booth. Two television cameras were trained on his face, there to catch every expression, milk every moment. The noise in the stadium grew louder. The final votes were coming in. He was neck and neck with Spain, and then a roar. There were too many people in the way, obscuring the illuminated scoreboard. Andreas stood on his seat to find out what was happening. A wave of excitement fluttered towards them and then everyone around them erupted, jumping on the spot, hugging each other, shouting 'Opa!' at the tops of their voices. An exuberant cheer, and fittingly also the title of his song.

And just in that millisecond, time stopped and a bubble of silence fell around Sakis. He felt his world shift, stepping from one reality to another. There would be no more panicking to pay his rent each month! No more grimy little clubs, with sticky floors and acrid air. No need to write cheap songs with easy lyrics so customers, half-crazed with cheap whisky could sing along at three in the morning. Now he would be surrounded with quality musicians! There would be heavy, heartfelt sessions into the night, passionate composition, meaningful lyrics, like-minded people. He had arrived.

His hand raised to his mouth to cover his gasp of shock, his fingers exploring how one of his front teeth just slightly overlapped the other, his imperfection. Then his sphere of quiet burst and the moment rushed in on him again as hands pulled him. He stood, the milieu propelling him towards a walkway that led back to the stage. The crowd was cheering, screaming his name. A rain of silver petals caught in his hair, settled on his shoulders and dazzled his progress. A microphone was clipped on his shirt and he was centre stage, with twenty thousand people waiting in front of him and one-hundred-and-ninety-five million worldwide. There was no way he could swallow. Blinking, he momentarily froze. Then he sang and forgot the world.

The party started as the last note faded. He has no recall of leaving the stage, just of people, crowds and crowds of people around him. A new place, a large room. Andreas shouting something about America, nodding furiously, encouraging. Handshakes and hugs, kisses and glasses of bubbly wine. Then the clamouring masses parted as a man, not a big man, in fact a small and neat person, roughly the same age as him, slunk up to him slowly. There was a recognition, the face of a stranger he had always known.

'Is "Opa" typical of the songs you write?' he asked, using English as the common language. His accent was French. Sakis felt such a relief at the question. He started with an emphatic 'No,' and then babbled about his hopes of bringing Greek urban music to the forefront. The questioner's head nodded in approval, understanding.

'The working class undercurrent has always preserved and propelled traditional Greek music,' Sakis explained, and the interviewer's unshrinking gaze conveyed an understanding. He talked on and on until a handheld camera with a German logo was thrust between them and a new interview began amidst the clamour.

As Sakis tried to concentrate, another glass of Champagne was thrust into his hand and he glanced back at the man with the French accent. It's funny how some people just fit. You know it instantly; there is a rapport.

The German reporter gave the French man a nudge and grunted, 'Give us some room, Jules,' and waved his fluffy mic.

Jules. The name suited him. He had agreed on the purpose of music, of art in general, the power it has for the underdog, the repressed masses, the people who toil to keep countries on their feet.

The sounds of something poured, a teaspoon against china brings Sakis back to the present. If it were Andreas in the next room, he would have shouted a loud *Kalimera* by now. Maybe it is room service.

In those first hours of winning, the throng around clamoured for his attention. Reporters from more countries than he could name wanted to interview him, each with a handheld camera and fuzzy microphone. It was difficult to focus— he had drunk too much wine—so he just smiled his best photogenic smile, turning his head slightly for each camera, doing his best to hide the overlap of his front teeth as he waved to the black lenses. He would be on the cover of every magazine and tabloid in Europe tomorrow.

Andreas was mingling, talking to as many people at once as he could, no doubt seeking out the best opportunities, arguing the best deals.

He cannot remember much more. At one point, he was outside and he was shocked at how cold Kharkiv was, but the people around him didn't seem to notice and he sang to the moon and the crowd of people around him joined in. So cold. Returning inside, he felt the need to break away, find some space, and it was a relief to see Jules sitting in a corner with a free chair next to him.

'Coffee?' A voice comes from the next room. Sakis sits up so quickly he has to hold his head. It is Jules.

'Coming.' His own voice sounds hoarse and feels as though a dozen razor blades have sliced through his tonsils. With a hand on his throat, he makes the effort to stand. The room swims. He is naked.

'Shall I bring it in?' Jules asks. His accent seems more pronounced today.

'No!' The word rasps his larynx raw. With a hotel dressing gown around him, he goes out to face the world. The world in which he has won! His tread is light; his feet barely touch the carpet.

The room is more populated than he expects. Jules, with unbrushed hair that sticks out at all angles, is on one sofa that is piled with crumpled blankets. He has the t-shirt on he wore the night before. Andreas is there too, hovering next to the fireplace, carefully presented in his pressed suit and new shirt, and there is a lean man with perfect teeth, also in a well-cut suit, who stands with hands in pockets, expectantly. Sitting by the door, staring ahead, tense, as if he is expecting a riot at any moment is the big man who was introduced as the new bodyguard the night before.

On a small side table, there is a tray with a coffee pot and several cups. The low, central table is strewn with newspapers and magazines and his own face grins back at him from a hundred different angles. He laughs. He won! The words sound so good, hold so many promises. He says it again inside his head. 'I won!'

Jules hands him a cup of coffee and nods ever so slightly at the pile of blankets. Sakis nods back, an even smaller movement that accepts that Jules stayed the night on the sofa. He takes the small white-gold-rimmed cup on its delicate saucer. It is very designer and impractical to hold, with the edges of the saucer so upright. It could almost serve as a small bowl, and this reminds him he must ring up his neighbour to remind her to feed the cats. Where did he put his mobile?

He closes he eyes as he drinks. The scalding of his throat feels good, but the swallowing exacerbates the pain. He should never have sung in the cold night air.

'How do you feel, my boy?' Andreas shouts in his excitement. 'We did it! Or rather, you did it! You are a global sensation—look at the reports!' He flourishes the magazine in his hand. 'We'll be rich! You, my friend, are famous…' Andreas puts down the periodical to pour his own drink, all his movements exaggerated, full of energy.

Sakis does not reply. He needs to wake a little more slowly.

'Right,' Andreas begins once armed with coffee. 'When you go back to Athens, I have arranged for you three television interviews and a press conference over two days and then, you can gather a few things and fly next Friday…' He is interrupted by a knock on the door. The bodyguard opens it a crack, then wider to admit a uniformed maid holding two bunches of flowers. On silent feet, she crosses the room and adds these to a table between the heavily draped windows that is already overflowing with floral offerings. On inspection, the cards are not from individuals but from the other countries. The largest bouquet is from Spain, who he beat by only two points! The UK has sent red, white, and blue roses. The Netherlands has sent green carnations and tulips. Italy has sent silk flowers—very stylish!

Outside the windows, the sky is a pale blue. The sun is sharp but the people hurrying on the streets are wrapped up in coats, hats, and scarves. Back in Greece, today will be another scorcher. If he were there, it would be a good day to go to the beach and lay motionless under an umbrella and allow his body to fight off the demons of the drink. He needs time to become an active member of the world again.

'Sakis, are you listening?' Andreas barks.

'What?' The impractical cup is shaking slightly in its saucer. Jules takes it from him, refills it, and offers it back. Sakis thanks him. There is no eye contact. Jules seems as half-awake as he is.

'America, Friday!' Andreas says as if it is something he is repeating.

'What?' Sakis asks, wondering if there are any pain killers. Maybe he should just go back to bed.

As if he has spoken his thoughts aloud, Jules conjures from nowhere a packet of Paracetamol tablets and pops two out of the blisters. Jules' fingernails are rough, as if he bites them, as he places the pills in Sakis' palm. Two fingers are stained with nicotine. There is something very real, grounding, and reassuring in his presence.

The tablets get stuck in the razor blades that are lodged at the back of his throat and it takes several swallows of coffee to encourage them to go down.

'You alright?' Andreas asks, his smile fading slightly.

'My throat feels like...' But he cannot finished the sentence. Every word feels like it is doing him harm.

'Well, order some honey and lemon or something. You have a press call in half an hour, okay?'

'Okay.' Sakis picks up his bouzouki, which is resting in its open case against the wall. His body moulds to accept the instrument's form and they become one. He strums a few chords, which soothe his soul but not his head. But then a new melody finds its way to his fingers. He plays it twice and then adds on a note. This is a song about dance; he can feel it. The chords that are forming, the melody that is coming have a heavy beat but are dreamy, like when he becomes lost in the rhythms of the *pentozali*, the Cretan war dance. When the ecstasy of being alive flows through his veins, his agility is brought to the forefront and he is swept into elations of the music's vigorous, sensual pulse.

'Conference room, half an hour,' Andreas reiterates loudly and leaves the room.

The press conference is crowded. There is standing room only and cameras and microphones are lined up on every available table space in front of him.

'Sakis, were you surprised to have won?'

To admit he is surprised would suggest he did not think his song was strong enough, which may be true but it is not something he is going to share. To say he is not surprised could be considered arrogant.

'I am delighted to have won,' he deflects. He takes a drink of water. The hot lemon and honey has soothed his throat somewhat, but it is still sore.

'Do you think Greece will benefit from you winning? Can Greece afford to host the contest next year?'

These are not questions he wants to consider. Why do they not talk about his music?

Andreas takes the questions, to his relief.

The door to the press room is open, with people coming and going as the conference proceeds. The noise is a constant hum, as many are translating everything that is said into hand-held Dictaphones.

'Is "Opa" typical of the songs you write?' The question cuts through the cloud of babble.

Sakis is not sure if it is the relevance of the question that pleases him, or the questioner. There, old-fashioned notebook in hand, press card around his neck, is Jules. He has changed his t-shirt and the one he now wears looks official. It bears the logo of a major European cult music paper that holds a certain gravitas in the subcultures of the music world. No wonder they got on so well.

'I think "Opa" has proved itself to be a song of the people,' Andreas begins emphatically.

'I prefer the songs I write that reflect more of Greek history. I am a big fan of *rebetika*, a term that comes from the word *rebetis,* which is very close to the word *mangas*. The *manga* was, and is, a proud working-class man. It is more than just about the music—it is about the character, dress, behaviour, morals, and ethics all associated with this subculture. The working peoples' voice.' Sakis can feel the passion swelling his chest and the rasping in his throat is ignored.

Jules scribbles furiously, smiling to himself, nodding.

'Of course our roots are important in our music. That is what this competition is about. But Greece is now part of modern Europe and "Opa" reflects this well,' Andreas interrupts, and before he has finished speaking, he points to another member of the press who has his hand raised. It is the turn of a new questioner. Jules has had his moment.

After the press conference, there is a lunch. After that, a television interview, and then a cocktail party, followed by dinner and the inevitable party. An endless bombardment of people ask trivial questions. After that one question from Jules, no one seems actually interested in his work, his song writing, his passion. Sakis accepts every glass of champagne offered. He also accepts that this is the reality of the fame he was seeking. It is a pale shadow of his dream. He spends the whole day half cut, wondering what he has done.

The following day, there are more parties. The pain in his throat has grown worse and he speaks as little as possible. Jules is around sometimes, and sometimes not, depending on each event. But he is in his hotel suite when the day is done, offering him a sense of grounding, something real, something that agrees with his soul. They talk of the deeper aspects of his music, what he is trying to say, the sense of community that maybe no longer exists that he is trying to evoke back to life. They continue to talk and talk into the night, his voice growing fainter and fainter until Jules forbids him to talk anymore and makes him a drink of lemon and honey.

Sakis yawns. It's been a long two days and his forehead is throbbing and hot.

'All right if I crash on your sofa again?' Jules asks. It doesn't need an answer.

Athens

'Oh, there you are.' It is Jules' voice. Where is he? His brow is mopped with a damp cloth that smells of lavender. 'You've had a rough few hours.'

The shadow of the window on the ceiling is familiar. He is at home. But how long has he been here? And why is Jules here?

Harris pushes her soft, furry, two-tone nose in his face, incessantly meowing for attention, her wide eyes on the edge of panic until she receives a caress. Ginger Eleftheria is weighting down his legs, his loud purrs drifting in the still room.

'You were out for the count for a while there. You have a fever,' Jules says. The cream curtains are drawn but the sun finds its way between the threads to spread a mist of its rays in the room.

He knows he has a fever. He is burning up.

'Is Andrea here?' There is a recall of Andreas and a woman with a stethoscope around her neck.

'No, he left hours ago. But you'd better heed what the doctor said and stop talking.'

'*Gamoto*!' Sakis hisses. This is such bad timing. He needs to get out there, take his bow, find his way to the serious musicians. He has his 'pass' of winning now; he needs to use it while it is still valid. The world is fickle.

'He said it's laryngitis, a virus, but my guess is all that partying didn't help.' Jules leans out the window to smoke a cigarette. The sun streams in around him and the heat rushes into the air-conditioned room.

'What do you think?' Sakis asks hoarsely. 'You think Andreas can keep the momentum up if I am off the scene?' But he cannot wait for the answer. His eyes must close.

There are no shadows on the ceiling when he wakes again. The room is dark except for a lamp on his desk where Jules sits typing away on a laptop whilst thumbing his way through a pile of magazines and newspapers. His face in the moment of joy when he won is all over the covers.

'Ah, you are awake. How you feel?' Jules stops typing.

'Better.' But his throat denies this. At least the throbbing in his head has gone.

A damp cloth is dabbed across his brow.

'Life shows no favours,' Jules states, getting up and going through to the tiny kitchen. He returns with a bowl of something steaming. 'Here you go. The market here is good, yes?' But it's not a real question.

'Thanks.' Sakis takes the bowl. 'It smells good. What are you writing?' What he really wonders is what is Jules doing here. Somehow it is not a question he feels he can ask when food is being provided. In any case, Jules pre-empts him.

'My paper's asked me to do an in-depth article on you. I told them a bit about you and they thought it would interest our readers.' He laughs as if the idea is ridiculous. 'You know: "The real musician behind the popular song,"' he adds as he goes back into the kitchen and returns with his own bowl of soup, into which he pours cream from a carton. He holds the carton out to Sakis, who pulls a face. He prefers to taste the vegetables.

'Truth is, when you got sick, Andreas made me an offer. He needed to keep milking your win. You know this expression of the English, to milk?' Sakis nods. 'There was no one to take care of you. So we made a deal. If I came back to Athens with you, then he would open doors for me when you go to America. You've heard of the American magazine *Urban Unchained*, right?'

Sakis looks up from dipping his spoon in his bowl. He knows *Urban Unchained*—who in the music world doesn't?

'I intend to be a journalist for them. So if Andreas can open some of the doors to musicians, then I will make sure I write what *Urban Unchained* likes to print. Meanwhile, I am capitalising on spending this time with you.' He does not drink his soup quietly.

Sakis had not expected such open honesty or steadfast ambitions from him. With his skin-and-bone frame holding up cheap, overwashed t-shirts and his not-very-recently cut hair, Sakis had sort of categorised him as—well, if he was honest, after he found he had spent the first night freeloading on his sofa, he had considered him a bit of a drifter despite working for such a solid European magazine. This new perspective makes much more sense about why they get on so well. They are as determined as each other.

'By the way, there are still reporters camped outside on the pavement waiting for you, you know?' Jules continues, almost in the same breath. 'And a line of girls with banners and slogans addressed to you. They call your name and wear t-shirts with your picture on.'

21

This is accompanied with a gentle laugh. 'I think you disappearing from the limelight so suddenly has increased everyone's interest.' With this, he drains his bowl, forsaking his spoon.

The phone rings. Jules offers to answer but Sakis feels bored with being ill so long, so he answers himself. It is Andreas.

'Right, Sakis, don't speak, just listen.' Sakis puts the phone onto speaker so he can put it down on the bedside table. 'I have recycled the films of you being interviewed in the Ukraine. I am going to get some of them edited to make them look like they are new clips, and I've dug some of your older interviews up and I am getting several press releases out there. So far, I have kept the momentum going. I mean, when you hit America, you may be there for some time, so the Greek public will have to get used to just getting snippets of your life anyway. The American deal, I have managed to push back for a weeks. If you are not recovered enough to sing, which of course you will be by then, they may be able to push it back for a further week or maybe two, but I wouldn't count on it.'

Sakis grunts in response.

'Now, the doctor said to get you out of the pollution, so I have booked you and Jules a couple of hotel rooms out of Athens, away from it all. She seemed to think the air quality was an important factor. I found a hotel down near that village where I think you said your *yiayia* used to live?'

'Near Saros?' Sakis asks, the surprise evident in his voice. It has been a long time since he was there. The last time was, well when was it? He must have been about eleven. No, he went back later. But he did not like the way people responded to him, what they called him. He was a nobody down there in the shadows of his baba.

'Yes, that's the one,' Andreas answers him. 'The hotel is between Saros and the village, a bit nearer the village, I think. It should be alright. They have hire cars; it's by the beach. Anyway, if you feel well enough to travel, I can send the car tomorrow. It's an hour and a half drive. What do you think? Can you manage that?'

Sakis would like to refuse to go. He would like to bound out of his flat and just enjoy his win, make the most of it. The longer time passes, the more he will be forgotten. But his rasping throat, aching limbs, and overall weakness give him no option.

'I guess.' Well, what else can he say?

'Can you put Jules on?'

'I am here,' Jules says.

'Oh, okay, Jules. Keep spooning that soup down his throat. I appreciate all you are doing. Keep me informed.' And the line clicks to a purr.

The Hotel

The beach seems to stretch endlessly in one direction and curves around the bay towards Saros the other way. The water is so blue, so alive, that if he wasn't standing there in person, he would think someone had tinted the whole scene. The sand is almost white and the occasional grain reflects the sun like a mirror, shimmering in the heat. There is a small beach bar covered with crispy brown palm leaves and a man in its shade is wiping glasses, slowly, as if there is never a need to rush. The pace of life in the half hour since they arrived has kicked back to a lazy amble. It seems a natural pace for Jules. As for Sakis, well he is still struggling with the virus. He has no energy at all.

'You want a drink?' Jules asks as Sakis lowers himself onto a sunbed and looks around. There is a pink-skinned family who has pulled four sunbeds together further along, and there is a very brown-backed sunbather who has not opened the square umbrella over his lounger nearer the bar. After the mayhem of Kharkiv, which was the last time Sakis was out in public, the place feels deserted.

'Yeah, something cool, with ice.' Sakis rubs his throat.

Jules returns with two tall drinks.

'Bartender told me that they are on him. He recognised you.'

Sakis looks over and the bartender raises the glass he is wiping in salute.

'Interesting bloke,' Jules continues. 'Quit a steady job in a bakery and took up this bar job to give himself time.'

'Time for what?' Sakis leans back. The heat of the sun kissing him all over, massaging his throat, works through the knots in his aching limbs.

'He's taken up the clarinet. He said something about each village tries to put on the best *panigyri*. What's a *panigyri*?'

'Like a party, a festival. Each village has a saint and each year, they celebrate the saint's day with music and lots of food. My *yiayia's*,' Jules frowns, 'grandmother's village has always been in competition to put on a better *panigyri* than Saros town, even though it is so much smaller.' Sakis hasn't thought about this for years. The village usually only conjures images of his baba. His big, larger than life baba. The man who eclipsed him no matter what he did. This memory is suggesting the village has also had a different influence. He always thought his musical inspiration had come from Pireaus.

'Ah, so an influence, then?' Jules asks.

'Never thought of it.' Sakis closes his eyes. 'My baba took me out of the village when it was time for me to start school. Said I needed a man's upbringing. Whatever that means. It was probably a joke and didn't mean anything, knowing him.'

'So you went to school in Pireaus. Was the school musical?'

'Baba stuck around for a few years but when I was ten, he decided I was old enough to cope by myself. He would go off for two and three months at a time with work. Said if I wanted anything, I should go to his best friend's wife. They lived in the same block. She liked to cook. I didn't complain. But on the weekends, I was in heaven. "Ah, we can't leave the little doll here by himself. We will take him," Antonis would say. "He's a child. He is too young," Antigone would answer. "Take him for the music," Roula would say and it was decided because Antigone could not be bothered to argue.'

Sakis pauses to recreate the scene in his head and take a sip of his drink. It is a while since he has thought of all this in detail.

'So they would be all dressed up, him in pointed shoes, slicked hair, his jacket only over one shoulder, and she would be in her tight red dress with its lace-trimmed skirt and they would swagger their way through the back streets, turning heads. When we reached the tiny bar, they walked like royalty to their table.' The images reappear in his mind so easily. The bars were little more than narrow rooms that opened onto the street with cobbled floors and unpainted walls. There would be five rough wooden tables at most, and a makeshift bar, the musicians crammed into a corner. If the sun was shining, the doors were folded back so the bar spilled onto the street, and in winter, they were pulled tight and the cavern filled with cigarette smoke and the heat of bodies. The other men, also in pointed shoes, long moustaches, and striped suits, acknowledged Antigone and Antoni's entrance with a lift of a cigar, a raise of a glass, and he would feel so important simply by association.

'We would eat all together. The music would play. Then after an ouzo or two, if the music took his fancy, Antigone would stand, and like a, how you say, a Spanish fighter...'

'A matador,' Jules offers.

'Yes, this, like a matador, his spine so straight it almost curved backward, he would reach out his hand to his wife. She would stand

28

slowly, refusing his hand and circle him, each foot kicking out as she stepped and then they would dance.'

'You Greeks, you like to dance.'

The sun has moved and Sakis' face is no longer in the shade of the umbrella, but the direct heat on his throat feels good, so he keeps his eyes closed and does not move.

'Yes, we like to dance. But this was not like the dancing that is taught in schools, passed down from parents to children. This was improvised and had a menace to it, often a fight between the man and woman, for dominance.'

The first time he saw such dancing, he was afraid. Its raw sexuality, the woman standing up to every move made by the man, scared him. In traditional Greek dancing, the onlookers often drop to one knee and clap in time to encourage the display. But with this dancing, the bar was silent except for the sound of the music and the pointed shoes and heeled slippers against the cobbles. They commanded the room. No one got up, no one entered. No drinks were served until they had finished. And all this time he sat, not daring to move, on a small, hard chair by the bouzouki player. As the player's fingers moved and strummed, he would wink at Sakis and nod at his baba's friends, presuming they were his parents.

The excitement he felt as a boy is in his veins again. Maybe he will return to his room and play his own bouzouki for an hour or two. But first, he must complete his story for Jules.

'When they finished, they would be bought many drinks, but, the most exciting part for me, the musician would pull my stool in front of him, put the bouzouki in my lap, and reach his arms around me to guide my fingers. I would play, or thought I was playing, to cries of bravo and comments such as, "The boy's a boy, but he's also *manga*," and I felt I belonged.'

Sakis turns to Jules to see if he understands what he is saying, the importance of the excitement. Jules is smiling and scribbling furiously in his notebook.

'Are you making notes on this?' Sakis asks.

'Sure,' Jules say languidly and puts his pencil down to rest. Neither of them say anything for a while. Sakis' desire to go and practice subsides as a stillness takes him over.

'Nice spot, this,' Jules remarks and as Sakis looks over to him, he sees his eyes are closed.

Sleep plays its usual trick and when Sakis opens his eyes again, the family of four has been replaced by a couple, and the man with the brown back is now three very pale girls with blond hair. A young woman is sitting at the beach bar and the bartender has hold of her hand and is leaning as far over the counter as he can to steal the occasional kiss. Sakis' face pulses hot. He has caught the sun.

'How you feeling?' the ever-vigilant Jules asks.

'Not aching so much, but my throat is still raw.'

'You want another drink?'

'In a while. I just dreamt we were in a bar without air conditioning in Paris. Are you from Paris?'

'They say I was born in a place called Etaut, up in the hills near Spain.'

'How do you mean "they say"?'

'Raised in an orphanage. Toulouse. Ran away and lived in Montauban, Limoges, Orleans, and finally Paris.'

'How old were you when you ran away?'

'Don't know. Don't know how old I am now.'

'What made you run?'

'I met a group of traveling musicians from Germany. They were colourful and free. I became one of them, but I am not for playing music. My skill, they decided, was cooking and later, I decided, it was writing. I wrote a piece about them and sold it to a Paris paper. They were furious, but they drank the wine I bought with the money.' Jules clips his words. He is taking no joy from the memory. 'What was your papa like?'

'Baba? He was bigger than life. So big that I felt I had to do something great to live up to him. I have felt this all my life. A pressure. He was a *manga*. A true working class *manga* from Pireaus, with the pointed shoes, the striped suit, the long mustachio, a wide sash belt to hide the knife he carried there. He would wear his jackets on one shoulder, leaving the other arm dangling like a cape or a shawl.'

The only way to really explain his baba would be to tell Jules one of his exploits. But if he does, he risks over-shadowing all he, Sakis, has achieved, reducing himself to nothing more than his baba's son again. But maybe not. Maybe Jules has more insight, maybe he himself has outgrown all that now. Maybe this is a chance prove all that is behind him. After all, he has won! He is known worldwide now. Besides, there is also something very comforting in talking about his baba.

'He was a big man, physically. His chest was so big, he had to get shirts made specially. He grew up diving for sponges. He could hold his breath the longest of any of the boys, so he got the bigger sponges and became known locally. By the time I was a boy, he was already diving on oil rigs, underwater welding.' There is not even a glimmer of awe from Jules, and this gives Sakis the courage to continue. 'The work he did paid well and the boy from a poor family became a man with money, but he never forgot his roots. He had no desire to spend his time with the wealthy. Like I said, his apartment was in a run-down area of Pireaus.'

'It sounds like you admired him.' Jules turns onto his stomach to tan his back.

'I did. But also... Let me tell you one tale.'

'Okay,' Jules mumbles.

'He was working on a rig off the coast of Africa and a group of them had shore leave. As it was too far to come back to Greece, he and his friends took a room in a coastal town. A town where a major river met the sea and inland was a network of marshes and tree-covered waterways. Tropical.' Sakis sits up to suck up the last of his drink and then he too lies on his front.

The sun is so high, the umbrella is casting little shade.

'So my baba decides it would be fun to rent a boat and explore the waterways. They took beer and food and the five of them got in a boat, Baba steering the, er, what is it called, oh yes, the outboard motor.'

Jules has his head turned towards him, one eye open, listening.

'They set up one waterway and it narrows to nothing, so they retreat and try another. After a while, one of the men declares that they are lost but my baba says he knows where they are. After another hour, the man who thinks they are lost is beginning to panic and he talks some of the other men into believing that they are lost, too. So Baba stops the boat to talk to them, calm everyone down. As he is speaking, the man who was panicking opens his eyes wide and he points, with his mouth hanging open but with no sound coming out.

'Baba turns to see what he is pointing at and, swimming towards the boat, just visible above the thick water, are the spines of the back of a crocodile. The man who was pointing finds his voice and lets out a scream. One of the other men throws himself over the far side of the boat as the crocodile rears out of the soup and with an open mouth goes for the men. The animal lands half in the boat, snapping and trying to find its feet. Everyone is screaming. Another man has flung himself overboard and is swimming for the shore…'

Sakis waits for the customary gasp, but Jules is silent, just the one open eye watching him as he speaks.

'The man under the animal has frozen rigid but my baba, from his cloth belt around his waist, draws out his dagger and throws himself on top of the crocodile. He gets his arm around its neck and throws himself onto his back, pulling the creature over so it is belly up. Then he slits the beast's neck from jaw line to jaw line.'

Sakis props himself up on one elbow and mimes the slitting of his own throat with his free hand, with an appropriate noise. Once his second ear is reached, he flops back down on the sun bed.

'He then gathers up his friends and they motor back to town with the crocodile still on board, which my baba sells for its skin, and he takes the men for a night on the town with the money.'

Sakis waits for the customary gasp, or cheer, or laugh of relief but none come.

'He was known as "Costas the crocodile killer" after that, and I became the son of Costas the crocodile killer. It is, was, a very hard act to follow.'

They lay in silence for a while, the sound of the sea at their feet. Laughter from the bar.

'Could he sing?' Jules asks finally.

'He saved five men's lives!' Sakis retorts.

'Did he make people happy?'

'He killed a crocodile.'

'Does that make the world a better place?'

He could get very used to having Jules around.

Saros Town

The following day, his throat feels a little better. Not first thing, but about an hour after he wakes up, he is aware that swallowing is no longer painful and that his limbs do not ache quite so much. But he does still feel like he has no energy.

Maybe going somewhere for the day will help, doing something that will ignite his spirit.

'Jules, you want to go into Saros?'

They have just finished breakfast in the courtyard of the hotel. The whitewashed walls are splashed with brightly coloured flowers. Each table has its own umbrella and the fine gravel under their directors chairs crunches quietly when they stand to go to the buffet for more coffee.

Jules is tearing at his third croissant and dipping it in his coffee.

'These are good, considering they are Greek and not French,' he says with a smirk.

'There is a sign there that says they are from a bakery in the village.'

'Coffee's good, too. Is that from the village, too?' He is teasing now.

'So, do you want to go?'

'To Saros town? Sure why not, if you feel alright.'

Sakis goes to top up his coffee. In the magazine rack by the buffet table, there is a journal with his face on the cover.

'It was good, wasn't it?' a voice beside him says as he takes out the paper and looks at the cover. It is all about the competition. 'The contest, it was good. We won!' The woman is wearing a sleeveless floral dress and an apron. She is unloading fresh mounds of toast from her tray into the rack. She is small in stature and there is an agelessness about her.

'Yes, we won.' The woman gives him a long, hard stare. Any minute, she is going to recognise him. He smiles in anticipation.

'You remind me of someone,' she says. He doesn't give her a clue, but he holds the magazine facing toward her, two smiling Sakis. 'Ah, I know who you remind me of, are you from round here? You have a look of …'

Sakis does not want to know. She may be ageless but she is old enough to have known his baba. She is about to take away his hard-fought-for identity and transform him into 'The Son of Costas the Crocodile Killer.'

'No. I am from Athens,' he says and turns away, taking the magazine with him to his table.

He watches her as he sits, already feeling bad about being so rude. The woman goes back to filling the basket with toast and adds more pots of jam to the depleted basket, picks up a dirty knife someone has left by the yoghurt, and leaves the courtyard, flashing him a smile despite his discourtesy.

Inside the magazine is a re-hashed interview that he did a couple of years ago for a very small paper. Andreas is hard at work. He will ring him today.

'Okay, let's go.' Jules wipes his mouth on his linen napkin.

The taxi drops them on the harbour's edge in Saros.

'Wow!' Jules draws out the exclamation. 'That is some sight.' He is looking out into the bay, where the old island fort floats on glistening blue water that moves like oil.

'That's the Bourtzi,' Sakis says as he pays the driver.

'Why would anyone put a fort out in the middle of the sea?'

'Well, there was an island there, a rock. To guard the entrance to the harbour, I suppose. You want to go across?'

'Yes, why not?' Jules runs his hands through his hair. He is not one for using a brush.

Further along, a sign on the far side of a big tarmacked jetty informs them that it is collapsing into the sea and that cars may no longer be parked there. Moored to this jetty is a fishing boat that has been adapted for carrying passengers. A plywood cabin has been cobbled together to enclose the planking around the boat's edges, which have been given vinyl fabric cushions. There is a handwritten sign on the pier, leaning against the hull, scraping its presence into the woodwork. It reads "Bourtzi, every half an hour. If you miss the last one back, you will have to stay the night."

There is no one around.

'Bourtzi. What does that mean?' Jules asks.

'It's the Turkish name, left over from when they occupied Greece. It means "Tower."' A seagull calls overhead. 'Later, Bourtzi and all of Saros was fortified by the Venetians because of pirates. You will see when we get across. Well, you won't see because it's not there now, but there were three floors with movable stairs. To confuse the invaders.' Sakis takes a moment to think. 'Like the Harry Potter film.' He chuckles.

Jules doesn't laugh. He looks out to the island and nods seriously, which brings Sakis back to his topic.

'After the Turks, it housed the guillotine. And the executioners. To have the executioners living in the town was considered bad luck, but they had to live somewhere.'

At one point, a set of steps leads down to the sea. Jules sits on the pavement, his feet on the top step, watching the fish in the clear water.

'It was a boutique hotel in the sixties,' Sakis finishes.

A boy with a hooded sweatshirt approaches, holding out what looks like a small plant pot, begging for money. His hood is pulled up and covers what looks like a very bad haircut. His clothes are filthy, with fresh black smudges across his shoulders, and his shoes have no laces. Jules searches his pockets but finds nothing. The boy slouches.

'But most importantly, it is now a place where part of the Saros music festival is held.' Sakis feels he should tell the dirty gypsy boy to leave, but Jules pats the floor next to him and the boy sits down, the two of them looking into the water.

'The boat man is taking his time to come,' Sakis says impatiently.

'You wait for the boat?' the dirty boy says in Greek. Sakis nods. Jules looks up from the fish to watch them talking.

'What did he say?' Jules asks in English.

'English,' the boy says. 'You wait boat?' His accent is thick.

Jules chuckles, a quiet sound, a private amusement.

'Yes,' he answers.

'I Bobby.' The boy pats his chest and then bends forwards between his knees, reaching into the water with his pot to scoop up a large piece of swollen bread that has been thrown for the fish from one of the harbour-side cafés. Draining the water away, the boy fishes out the doughy mess and presses it between his fingers. It disintegrates and the slime dribbles into the sparkling surface and sinks, turning the water slightly milky. The few fish that are there rush to the cloud, and new fish swim in from further away. They quickly become a ball of swirling, glistening scales, and the cloudiness clears as the particles are eaten. Bobby shows no surprise at this performance. The water is soon crystal clear again and the boy looks at his fingers, which are covered in a doughy slime. He brushes them together and then dips his flowerpot in the water again and pours the water first over one hand and then the other.

'You wait long time,' he says to Jules. It does not sound like a question.

'Half an hour, Bobby,' Jules informs him. 'You go school?'

'No.' He must be about nine or ten years old.

'Your mama?'

'I no have.'

'You alone?'

'Yes.'

'Hm.' Jules nods as if he understands. The two of them stare at the water in silence. Sakis would like to join them, but the two of them sitting there happened so casually, and if he sits too, it will not seem natural. He shifts his weight from one foot to the other and swallows, testing his throat for soreness. It is alright. Not great, but alright. He is feeling a little tired. Perhaps coming to Saros was overdoing things.

'No boat,' Bobby says suddenly. *'To ftiaxnoun.'* He reverts to his Greek.

'Ftiaxnoun. What's that?' Jules creases his eyes closed against the sun and puts up one hand for shade as he looks at Sakis.

Sakis looks across the flat water. Now he notices the scaffolding around one side of the fort and the busy people.

'He says they are fixing it.'

'Oh.' Jules does not seem concerned. The boy stands, puts his flower pot under Jules' nose. Jules pulls his pockets inside out to show that he really does not have any money lurking there. Jules asks Sakis for some change.

He rummages in his pockets and takes out some loose coins and hands them to Jules, who puts them in Bobby's flowerpot cup. The boy shakes the coins gently against the pot's sides, smiles a grubby smile, thanks Jules in Greek, and walks away toward one of the cafés, flowerpot leading the way.

'That's a real shame we cannot go over.' Sakis sighs. 'I wanted you to see how it was when people lived and died for the causes they believed in. The events that inspired the traditional music. Greece when it was more real.'

'I think that was pretty real.' Jules speaks slowly and takes out a cigarette, lights a match against his thumbnail, and inhales deeply.

Sakis frowns.

'Bobby,' Jules clarifies. 'He was pretty real.' Then he stands.

'He was just a beggar boy, probably a gypsy, but could be Romanian, Serbian, Bulgarian. It's all the same these days.'

'He seems to be quite a character to me.' Jules looks out to the fort.

Sakis is not sure what Jules is trying to say.

'He was a character, and so?' This feels like the first time they have had a discord and with the slight tension, he feels the need to sit down all of a sudden. The ground has shifted.

'So nothing. His life is very real. His need to eat and survive its very real. He came here away from his home in Romania or Serbia, or wherever, and that is very real.' Jules looks him in the eye. 'I think if the boy were musical, he would write a song about it.'

Sakis looks after the boy.

'History in the making.' Jules pushes the point.

Perhaps he should have given Jules more change than he did to give to the boy.

'I am feeling not so good again. I know we have just arrived, but is it alright with you if we go back to the hotel?'

Jules shrugs, stands, and begins to meander in the direction of the car.

'Why did they put a car park by the harbour? So ugly,' Jules murmurs, picking tobacco from his lower lip.

'Not just ugly but dangerous.' The words come out more sharply than he intended. He'll not say any more, just let it slide. Jules won't ask.

'Why dangerous?' Jules asks as he kicks a small stone over the harbour's edge. It plops through the surface, creating a circular ripple that grows wider and wider on the oily surface. The stone itself oscillates side to side as it sinks slowly to the bottom. It lands and fine sand puffs up and mixes with the sea.

'Someone once put their car into forward gear when they meant to go backwards.'

'They went in, I guess,' Jules says coolly.

Sakis does not answer. He has never been told the story directly. Instead, he has picked up pieces here and there, put them together. She was angry. He had phoned and asked her to come into Saros to join him for a drink. But when she arrived, he started talking to some male friends. She had poured herself more wine from the jug, waiting to be given some attention. She had drunk more and more until when she stood, she was not steady. When he returned, the jug was empty. She had left, angry, and he remained.

'The next day, they called on everyone they knew, he and my *yiayia*, thinking that she had stayed with friends. They asked around for days,' Sakis says.

Jules looks at him sharply.

From the bits his *yiayia* had told him, no one knew where she had parked the car, nor of its relevance. The police were called. A search was made, house to house inquiries, and as time passed, they presumed she had just had enough and left. Gone to Athens to start a new life, maybe. But no one could really believe that she would do that and leave behind her baby son. It was a week or two later that someone casually mentioned that they may have been the last to see her when fumbling with the door, trying to get her key into the lock where she was parked with the bumper hanging over the harbour's edge.

'The police wanted to send a diver down to pull up the car. My baba volunteered.' Sakis stops walking. He should not have come to Saros. It was too much for him, and thinking about this isn't helping. It is not as if it does any good; he never even knew her. He was just a baby.

The water by the harbour's edge is so clear, he wonders why they did not see the car sooner. But further along, where she went in, it is much deeper and oil tends to collect there on the surface as the current turns.

Jules grinds his cigarette out with the toe of his flip flop and throws a lank arm around Sakis' shoulder, pulling him in. Sakis can feel the pulse of his friend's heart against his arm. He lets himself be steered to a bollard and Jules pushes him to sit down as he sinks, himself, into a squat. His baba told him the rest of the story for no reason one night in Pireaus, when the ouzo had flowed. His big strong baba terrified him with his tears and shaking shoulders.

'At first, the water was clear but as I let my body sink, it darkened, became misty.' That's how he began to tell it, just like that, out of the blue. Sakis had no idea to what he was referring.

'I felt the car before I saw it. I was sinking feet first and my foot hit the bumper. The whole thing was on end, its nose stuck in the sand, the exhaust pointing to the surface.' His baba took a big lungful of air and a cold chill crept over Sakis as he began to have an idea what he was talking about. But in his head, it is his baba's voice.

'Letting out some air, I sunk further, keeping my eyes fixed on the bottom. I traced down the edge of the car's roof with one hand, using it to pull myself deeper until I stood on the sea bed, the bonnet against my belly, and then I braced myself and looked up from my feet. There she was! As beautiful as I remembered her. She still had her seat belt on. Her skin was no longer that wonderful bronze colour that she went in the sun. She was white as marble.'

His shoulders shook, but there was no sound of him sobbing. Big tears ran down his face, dripping into his ouzo glass, clouding tiny patches of the spirit.

'Her eyes were closed as if she was sleeping. But one arm.' He stopped talking to release the saddest chortle. 'One arm waved to me. I knew it was the current but in a moment of madness, I could believe she was still alive. Then as the truth recoiled back, it made me lose my breath and I had to rush to the surface.'

Sakis pauses.

Jules' face has lost all colour.

'He had to attach the chains so they could haul her up. The police said, once the chains were attached, his job was done, but Baba insisted on travelling with her. Their last journey together, from the sea bed to the harbour side.' Sakis takes a big breath. Jules' hand is on his knee and Sakis takes hold of it for strength.

'He watched her as the car was slowly pulled up. Her hand still waving, her dark hair floating around her smooth white face. Baba surfaced first and then up came the car, up came Mama.' His grip on Jules' hand tightens.

His baba's voice became cold and emotionless when he got to this part.

'As the car came out of the water, the fullness of her face drained away and then, as if life wanted to cause the maximum pain, there before my eyes, as I watched, her face fell, slithered into the footwell, away from her bones, and her skeleton hung inside the seat belt, tendons and sinews where body and soul should have been.'

Sakis, dry eyed, stares out to sea, releasing his grip on Jules' hand.

'That's reason enough not to come back here,' Jules says quietly. 'Do you blame him?'

'Blame who?' Sakis has become lost in a stare, absent.

'The crocodile killer. Do you blame him for your mama's death?'

Glancing at Jules, he cannot look him in the eye.

'Can we go?'

'Sure.' Jules straightens up stiffly and offers Sakis a hand to stand.

They wait by the road's edge for a taxi. Sakis waves at the first to pass, but it does not stop.

'About a month after he told me this, I came home from school and he was drunk again. "Your *yiayia's* died," he said, straight out. The one last remaining soft piece of my world was whipped from under my feet, leaving a gaping hole that I thought I was going to fall down. She had been my mama from six months old till my baba took me to Pireaus, aged six. I waited for the drop, to find myself hurtling down an empty-sided chasm but before it came, he added, "She left you her house. Not me. You! Could she had stated more loudly that she blames me for your mama's death?" Then he gulped down another ouzo and the ground beneath me sealed over like concrete. Concrete beneath me, concrete round me. Encased. Quietly, I went to my room, packed a bag, and left without seeing him again. I was thirteen.'

As Jules nods with such exaggeration, his whole upper body rocks back and forth. He totally understands.

A taxi pulls up and the driver leans out of his open window. 'Where to?' he asks.

51

'The village hotel.' Sakis pulls himself together and points the direction as they climb in.

Back in the hotel room, he sleeps all afternoon and when he goes down to the beach bar in the evening, he finds Jules chatting to the barman as if he has known him all his life. He has a drink in his hand which he had no money to buy, so his new friend must be footing his bill, too. There are tables on the lawns and diners eat, watching the setting sun over the water. A clarinettist wanders from table to table playing a variation on a haunting traditional song. Sakis listens to the arrangement and his thoughts become engulfed in imagining how it could be improved. A totally new song comes to mind and he is tempted to return to his room, work it out on his bouzouki. But Jules sees him and raises his glass in salute, and then slides off his bar stool.

'Is this your "real" music?' he asks with half a crooked smile.

'Ah, he is trying. Just earning a living with variations,' Sakis defends. But as he listens, the clarinettist's skill becomes more apparent and he locks eyes with Jules.

'You see,' Jules says. 'He has just as much talent as you in his playing, but it was not he who won. It was you.'

Sakis frowns, not understanding the point.

'Maybe it is not the skill that makes people winner or famous. Maybe it is luck, or maybe,' and he smiles softly before he says this, 'it's your looks and because you are likeable.'

Sakis feels flattered by these words but also insulted, as if his musical skill were not enough.

'You cannot exclude that it might have been you character that got you chosen to, how you say, play for your country.'

'The word is "represent,"' Sakis says under his breath.

'Yes, it may be that you represent your country because you are thoughtful and kind and always on the alert to other peoples' feelings. That is our default, you and I. To be on alert for other peoples' feelings. That is what happens if a child is sent into the world on its own too young. It is a necessary skill to ensure its survival.'

Sakis tries to think of something to say, but nothing comes that he can use to change the path of the conversation.

'And it is important that someone kind and thoughtful won, because it is the people who win through history who write the history books. It is the people who are noticed that dictate the music that becomes "traditional." In this light, we can see that the traditional music that you are so passionate about is, maybe, not the music of the people but the music of the successful.'

'Why are you saying this?'

'The receptionist says there was a call from Andreas.'

'Oh, okay. I will go and call him.' Sakis turns to go back the way he has come, but stops and turns again to Jules. 'But what has what you just said got to do with that?'

'Call him,' Jules says and begins an idle walk back to the beach bar, where the bartender is still leaning over towards the seat Jules left, as if waiting for him to return. Sakis goes inside.

The girl in reception speaks English without an accent. She says he can either use the phone at reception or the one in his room. When he points to the reception phone, the girl, whose name tag says she is called Ellie, not only offers him the phone but also pushes her wheeled chair around to the side of the counter so he can sit in comfort.

'Hi Andreas, how is it going?'

'Hey hey, how is the winner!' Andreas seems full of energy and life after Jules and the laid-back feeling of the village hotel. Sakis feels tired just hearing his voice.

'My throat is better but I still feel tired.' It is a relief to speak Greek after all the English he has been speaking with Jules. He hasn't realised what hard work it is to think in English.

'That's good that your throat is better. Now, there is good news and not-so-good news.'

'Tell me!' Sakis sits up straight.

'Well, the not-so-good news is just temporary. Difficult, but temporary.'

'Just tell me.'

'Okay. I went to get some of your older photograph albums from your apartment, to use in the press releases, and your landlord informs me that you are two months overdue with the rent. I did try to argue with him but I am afraid he was adamant and he has packed all your things and moved you out. He wants his rent.'

'Did you pay him?' Sweat runs down from his temple.

'Well, here's the thing, Sakis. We have not actually made any money yet. I've been given bits and pieces for the videos of your interviews but that has gone on to re-editing some of your older interviews and various press material. Until you appear live somewhere, there's not much cash to be had. I have managed to keep things going and you are still big news, but the sooner you are back in action, the better.'

A deep heat sweeps across Sakis' forehead and then he feels cold. His flat is gone. He own musical sanctuary is no longer his. Oh my God. He no longer has a place to call his own! And what about the cats?

'So listen, this is what I have done.' Andreas talks quickly, not giving him time to speak. 'The boxes of your things that the landlord packed for you, I have put into my *apothiki*, where they can stay as long as it is necessary. But your cats were the problem. The cheapest solution I could find was to put them in their box and pop them on a train to go down to you in Saros. The hotel has agreed to pick them up for you. They should arrive later today.'

'I cannot have Harris and Eleftheria here in the hotel. Surely the hotel owner will forbid it. You cannot put them on a train; they will be terrified.' His throat is so dry now.

'I kind of knew that but I had no choice, Sakis. Where else would they go? Anyway, it's done. They are already on the train.'

Sakis' forehead feels clammy. Maybe he should have taken this call in his room after all, where at least he could lie down whilst speaking.

'The hotel owner has agreed to this?'

'Well, as I said, this is just a temporary problem. Once we get to America, we will be rolling in money. But meanwhile, you must have some relatives you can stay with down there.'

'Is there money to pay the hotel?'

'No, no, you are fine. Well, for tonight anyway. I called Stella, the hotel owner, and had a long chat with her. Such a nice lady, and I have paid half tonight's tariff already, and she says the cats are fine for the one night. You must have someone down there that you can stay with. After all, your family is from there, right?'

The receptionist is looking at him and frowning. She hurries through the arch to the courtyard where he and Jules had their breakfast and returns quickly with a glass of water.

As the liquid rushes down his throat, he feels such gratitude.

'Thank you.' He looks her in the face.

'You are welcome.' Andreas sounds full of energy again down the phone.

'Not you, Andreas.' He almost swears down the phone. 'Where am I to sleep tomorrow night?'

'Didn't your *yiayia* leave you her house? I'm sure you said something like that once. So if all else fails, you can stay there, no?'

'*Yiayia's* house? It is a village-style cottage and it has stood empty for the last fifteen years. The roof will have fallen in by now. Good God Andreas, you are my manager. You are meant to manage things. What kind of management is this?' As his voice raises, the sourness in his throat returns.

'Look, just stay there another couple of days because now I tell you the good news! That music label that wants you over in America, well I am negotiating with them to pay our tickets to get over. They are almost in agreement. Brilliant, eh? This time next week? You'll be good by then, right? Because they are lining up interviews on American TV. But until I have the tickets in my hand, stay there where you can live rent free in your *yiayia's* house. Because, and let's be honest, I can hear by the rough edge in your voice you are not ready to come to Athens for round after round of back-to-back interviews, are you?'

'Look, if that is what I have to do, then that is what I will do.'

Andreas sighs.

'Sakis, my friend. If you come up to Athens and do the interviews, sure we will have a little cash, but if it pushes your recovery back and that makes the American deal fall through, then we will have lost the big time. You want to lose the big time? Do you want to just be a big fish in the little pond in Greece or do you want to hit the really big time? New York my friend, New York!'

Sakis' eyes are closed. The throbbing in his head is fuzzing his thinking. What he needs is to lie down.

'Sakis, you still there?'

'Yes.' He sounds weary even to himself.

'Excuse me, are you Sakis in room 24?' A bellboy in an oversized suit piped in red approaches the reception desk.

'Yes.' Sakis needs all his strength just to speak now.

'I have a delivery for you. Sign here please.' A mewing sound can be heard as a board with an official paper is shoved under his nose, and he signs to take delivery of Harris and Eleftheria. The poor things are shaking, huddled together at the back of the cat box. They must be terrified.

'Sakis, Sakis you there?'

'Yes, Andreas, I am here. So are Harris and Eleftheria, both of whom are terrified.'

'Okay, well, stay there then and I will call you in a couple of days to tell you I have the ticket for New York City.' He can hear Andreas smiling as he says the American capital's name.

Saying goodbye is not worth the effort so he hands the phone back to Ellie, who hangs up for him. He manages to stand by steadying himself on the reception counter and with sliding feet, he makes his way back to his hotel room and all but falls onto the bed. The bellboy puts the cat carrier beside the bed and closes the door on his way out.

He sleeps solidly and only wakes when Harris begins to cry piteously the following morning. She either needs to go to the toilet or she needs feeding. Slipping into his jeans, he definitely feels a little better today. Which is just as well, as he has to find somewhere to stay. There is a note under the door.

'Maybe this is useful.'

Out in the corridor is a cat litter tray and a tin of cat food and another note in Greek.

'Ask at reception if you need anything else. Stella.'

Well, that's a kind start to the day at least.

He takes everything inside and after shutting the door and checking the patio window, he lets the cats out. Jules is in his narrow bed by the small bathroom and is snoring gently. Harris is very happy to be free and she sniffs around the cat litter tray before making very aromatic use of it. Eleftheria goes straight to the cup of water he has put down.

'God almighty, what is that smell?' Jules murmurs as he turns over. He opens his eyes long enough to make out the cats and the tray and then closes them again and pulls the thin cover over his head and turns to face the wall.

'Man, that's bad!' he groans.

After the cats have both eaten and drunk and used the tray, Sakis, sadly, puts them back in the tiny carrier. He has to open a window, the smell is so bad.

'Put it down the toilet, Sakis.' Jules turns back to face him again, throwing his covers off and stretching noisily.

Sakis lifts the tray. He cannot pour all the litter down the toilet; it will block. Perhaps if he fishes bits out with a wad of tissue.

'Oh man, that smells disgusting.'

'You know what, Jules? I don't need to hear this.'

Jules stops stretching and seems genuinely shocked. Then his high eyebrows relax and his face takes on a look of compassion.

'Ah, you spoke to Andreas last night.'

'How much did he say to you yesterday when I was sleeping?'

'Well, it was not what he said, really. More his tone of voice.'

'We need to find somewhere else to stay.' Sakis flushes the toilet and puts the tray by the window.

'You're joking?'

'I wish. He suggested that we go and stay in my *yiayia's* house.'

'Okay.' Jules pulls on his t-shirt. His jeans are scrunched from being slept in.

'How much money do you have? We will still need to eat.'

'Nothing, my friend. You?'

Sakis checks a compartment in his bouzouki case. 'Eighty euros.' He stuffs his hands deep into the pockets of his jeans. 'And some change. So we can either stay here another night, or we can eat for maybe three or four days.'

'What about America?' Jules sits on his bed and pushes a finger through the cat carrier's mesh to stroke Harris' nose.

'He says he will know in a day or two. I'm sorry, Jules. I know you were counting on Andrea and me to open doors for you. Right now, I would not be surprised if Andreas doesn't blow all our rides, as the Americans say.' His choice of cliché is meant to make them both smile, but neither of them does.

'Okay.' Jules wraps his finger around the cat's ear and pulls gently, and she turns her head to one side in bliss. 'Right.' He stands with energy. 'Let's go. We do not have to check out till eleven is it, or twelve, so leave the cats here and we can see if your grandmother's house is still standing, right?'

The net curtains at the windows cannot hold back the sun and the day's heat is already building in the room.

'Best put the cats in the bathroom. It will be coolest in there.' Jules picks up the basket.

The Village

The fluorescent pink shock of bougainvillea almost completely obscures the windows. In contrast, the tightly closed shutters sing out in blue peeling paint. In the surrounding walls of greying whitewash, brave plants struggle for footholds in the cracked surface, dried out in the full glare of the sun's heat. Pushing aside vine leaves, Sakis curls his fingers around the heat-warped edge of one of the shutters, but it is soon clear that no amount of pulling is going to open them. The front door has boards nailed across, so he tries round the back. The old wood looks as if it had moulded into the frame. Grass grows out of the decomposing wooden doorstep, still green in the shade it has found.

Sakis wipes his handkerchief across his sweating brow. His embroidered initials pucker the silk and break up the smoothing feel, and somewhere deep within him, an edge of annoyance stirs. The affluent display of his monogram dilutes the practically of the article. For the price of this hanky, which Andreas bought him as a gift just before the competition, he could have stayed another night in the hotel. How quickly things change.

'Someone must have a key.' Jules has not moved from the gate.

'Hang on. There is a shutter that is only held closed by the stone on the windowsill here.' He does not want to ask around to see who has the key. How soon would that result in him being recognised as The Son of Costas the Crocodile Killer? Too soon, that's for sure. No, if he can get in on his own terms, that would be best.

'The window will be shut, though.' Jules takes a cigarette from behind his ear and strikes a match on the gatepost.

Sakis lifts the stone off the sill and is not entirely surprised to find a key.

'There's a key,' he calls out but wishes he hadn't. It feels as if he has swallowed razor blades. His throat seems to have got worse again since talking to Andreas.

Jules folds his long arms across his stomach. Sakis thought he would have been enthusiastic about this sort of work. When he lived on the streets, he must have found his way into many a building for a good night's sleep. If he helped, they would probably get inside within minutes. But he does not seem interested. He is looking down the street at something. Sakis follows his gaze and watches a black cat slowly crossing the deserted road to another single-storey whitewashed cottage. The houses vary: some are squat cottages that give the appearance that they have been settling into the soil forever, and others are two-storey concrete buildings with wide balconies festooned with colourful plants and arched with bougainvillaea. Then there are the occasional old stone houses, bereft of their plaster and whitewash finish, windows and doors hanging at odd angles or gone completely. Hollow, lifeless eyes and gaping mouths sing of past, simpler times. They sit in untended grounds where chickens scratch in the dust. In the shade of a dark doorway, a donkey shuffles gently, its neck bowed and eyes closed in the heat.

Jules leans against the gatepost, the elbow of one arm resting on the wrist of the other, and feeds himself nicotine. Sakis wonders why he doesn't quit. He seems so practical and down to earth in so many ways, it is at odds with his character that he is conned by something so destructive

The key fits in the back door and turns easily. The door is stiff and resists Sakis' shoving it. He will have to really put his shoulder to it. It moves only slightly, with a sound of splintering wood, and now his shoulder throbs.

'Yes? Can I help you?'

The voice comes from behind him. At first, he sees no one but then from around the back of the neighbouring house, hitching his trousers over narrow hips with one hand, saunters a man holding a watering can.

'I just wanted to go in and look.' Sakis brushes dust from his shoulder.

'Ah, the curiosity of youth,' the man replies. 'But it's not for sale.' Sakis can feel the old man's pale watery eyes take him in at a glance and then, with a quick sideways glance, he absorbs the portrait Jules cuts by the gate. Even through his own eyes, they look like city people rather than villagers. A smile teases at the crinkled corners of the old man's mouth. 'Now if you want to buy something…' The old man steps to one side and raises his watering can to indicate the house he stands beside. There is no for sale sign and the place looks rather uncared for.

'Are you selling?' Sakis asks. It is more polite conversation than a real question.

The old man names an unreasonable figure and then chuckles. 'Everything is for sale at the right price, eh my friend?'

Turning back to the immovable back door, Sakis braces himself to give it one more really hard shove.

'I am going to have to stop you there, my friend.' The watering can is put down, the sleeves are pushed up. Jules grinds out his cigarette and exhales the last of the smoke, straightens himself, and looks ready to deal with any trouble.

'Perhaps it is no business of yours.' Sakis does not say it with any venom. It is just a flat statement.

'Now, now, friend. We do not come to Athens and try to break into your houses. You would consider that unreasonable.'

'To be honest, I would consider my neighbour's business none of my own.' Again, no venom, pleasantly said, no antagonism. His eyes feel like they want to close; his throat is feeling sore again. He should stop talking.

'And that is the difference between city life and village life, perhaps. Here I keep an eye on it for the owner. Now lock the door and put the key back.'

It is not a request, it is a statement.

'He is the owner,' Jules says, stepping towards them.

Why did Jules have to say that? Sakis sees the rest of how he planned his days instantly evaporate, the chance of returning to the hotel and taking a nap gone. At least for the next few hours, the need to rest his voice will be given very little consideration. He blinks slowly as he seeks some inner strength for what is to come.

The old man looks him over again and his shoulders drop in recognition. A smile splits his face and sets his eyes dancing. Sakis knows he will not be able to maintain his distance, he will be pulled in by the old man's animation, by his happiness, and Sakis will respond by doing whatever it takes to keep the smiles from fading. He is always driven to please others, it seems. He tries to be selfish, think of his own needs, but once he has pleased someone else, it is like an internal urge to keep them pleased. It is his nature, and what he is good at. He is so good at it that it has, bizarrely, become his career. After all, was he not chosen over others to perform in the competition because he ingratiated himself to the committee? He flirted slightly with the ladies who responded quickly to his looks, and he took on the role of the alpha male, as they call it, with the men. His desire to please and be accepted is at the very core of his music. He sings of days gone by when the world was smaller and people took care of each other. He writes the jolly melodies that people love to sing along to. But once in a while, like now for instance, it would be really good to know how to be selfish. He needs to put the recovery of his voice first so he can fulfil his New York obligations at the end of the summer.

'Sakis? I thought you seemed familiar!' The old man steps up to the low wall that separates the two gardens and offers his hand. 'Ah, look at you all grown! I still think of you as this high, singing to the tortoises. Do you remember?' The pitch of his voice has risen. A white-haired lady in a housecoat appears behind him, wiping her hands on a tea towel.

'Who's this? Sakis?' the woman asks.

He nods. The smell of smoke tells him that Jules has lit up another cigarette and that he is now standing closer behind him.

'Ah my boy.' The old woman grabs Sakis over the wall and clinches him in a bear hug that has more strength than he expects.

'Lovely to meet you, but I'm afraid we really need to go,' Sakis says, but not very loudly, over the woman's shoulder. The hug has not finished and now the old man is patting him on the back at the same time. A second, younger man, about his own age, comes out of the house.

'No! Sakis!' this newcomer shouts, and as his mama, or is it his *yiayia*, releases her grip, he pulls Sakis in for his own hug.

'Anna!' the old woman calls across the street. 'Anna!' she calls again and in the house opposite, a front shutter opens, a flash of the sun's rays reflecting off the window, orange and startling. 'It's Sakis, Costas' son.' The window is closed again and, in less than a minute, the neighbour is padding across the road in lime green fluffy slippers.

He has been here less than a minute and already he is named as his baba's son.

'Katerina!' The woman in fluffy slippers squawks as she rolls towards them. The shutters in the house next to hers open, eyes flash, a nose catches a ray of sun, and then the window bangs closed again and a thin lady in a shabby housecoat hurries with quick birdlike movements towards them.

Everyone is talking at once, all trying to hug him, shake his hand, pat his back. Their warmth takes him by surprise but then again, it doesn't. His memories of living with his yiayia when he was a boy are full of feelings of being loved, cherished, and accepted. But most importantly of all, those first few years before his baba killed the crocodile, he was his own person, little Sakis, with nothing to prove and no pressure to impress. Blissful days.

The neighbour's wife must have gone in the house, as she comes out again with glasses of water on a tray.

'Hold this, Thanasi,' she orders the man so she can wipe over the garden table before she arranges glasses and water jug on its sun-blistered surface. She invites everyone to sit down, pushing a cat off one of the padded seats, then scuttles inside to bring more chairs.

'He used to line the tortoises up and sing to them, do you remember, sister?' Thanasis is telling the group and addresses the woman as she returns with a folding chair. In the back of his mind, Sakis makes a mental note that they are siblings, not man and wife. In his mind's eye, he recalls the memory of the tortoises that he had all but forgotten. Now it comes back as if it was yesterday. He had his favourite faded, red shorts on, no shoes, no shirt. It was the day after his *yiayia* had cut his hair and he was still finding snippets and strands in his ears. *Yiayia* was sitting on her wooden chair, shelling peas under the wisteria that smelt so sweet and hummed with bees as he tried to teach the tortoises to sing in harmony, turn them into a choir. He sang each part to them in turn in the thin strains of his four-year-old voice and encouraged them to copy, acting as choirmaster.

'Who would have thought, the son of Costas the crocodile killer, back here,' the old woman says. What was her name? Thanasis and… Thanasis, her brother who never married, didn't he breed donkeys? Yes, that's right, and his sister, who also never married. Dora! Yes, sweet Dora. Who, if his memory serves him correctly, made those red shorts for him on her pedal-powered sewing machine. How that treadle fascinated him as a boy.

'Ah Costas, he was some man! You dive like your baba, Sakis?' the woman with green fluffy slippers asks. He has no idea what her name is and does not remember her at all.

'No, Anna, he sings. Have you not seen him?' the bird-like lady says. Sakis smiles. The bird woman, what had the lady in fluffy slippers called her? Katerina, was it? Well whatever her name is, she recognises him and he immediately likes her. He opens his mouth to tell Katerina of his career, his unexpected win, when a deep voice speaks out.

'Sakis, you are a man now, eh! Not as tall as your baba, but all man now, eh?' The face is vaguely familiar. Thanasis takes a glass of water and pours the content into a pot brimming over with flowering geraniums. He refills it from a bottle of ouzo that has appeared from nowhere.

'It's good to see you.' Yorgos has broken away from chatting with Jules and he places a firm grip on Sakis' shoulder. They used to play together as children. Yorgos was Dora's nephew or godson, or something like that. *Yiayia* would have them sit side by side at her kitchen table, a glass of milk each, her home-baked biscuits piled on a plate in front of them as she sewed. The fire would cough smoke back into the room in the winter. In the summer, the house would smell of the incense she burnt for her dead husband, another smell for her dead parents, one for the saints.

The number of people around him grows, the name *Costas* on everyone's lips. Once or twice, someone mentions that he sings, but mostly tales are told again of his baba's boat trip in crocodile country. The slashing of the crocodile's neck becomes a split from throat to tail. The crocodile grows in size, the boat shrinks, the number of people saved increases, and hearty slaps on Sakis' back reduce him into being Costa's son once more.

There are so many people and so much fuss is being made that Sakis does not see the barbecue being lit. Nor does he notice women running back and forth to their houses, bringing meat to grill and wine to drink. Yorgos is over by a hydrangea bush offering a cigarette to Jules, who takes two and puts one in his mouth and one behind his ear. Something Jules has said has amused him and he is laughing heartily as he offers a light. The women fuss over Sakis, bring their daughters who are too old to be at school and too young to be married to stand shyly around the congregation's edge. More tales of his baba are told, some of which are new to him.

'Hey, you remember when he carried Theo's baba all the way back from Saros over his shoulder after a heavy drinking session?' Anna of the green fluffy slippers says and laughs as she holds out her glass to Thanasis for more ouzo.

'Ha, yes, and then there was the time he lifted a donkey for a bet and the donkey emptied its bowels,' Thanasis counters, and this is met with much laughter.

'What about the time he walked to Epidavros to see his sick uncle, what was his name, when his car was not working?' bird-like Katerina says. The response to this includes serious nods and murmurs and someone hands her a small glass of pale red wine. It seems there is no end to the tales, and each is accompanied by a slap on Sakis' back, as if he were the owner of the story. Each slap knocks a little more of the singer out of him. Jules is still talking and laughing with Yorgos, a glass of wine in his hand.

'Hey Yorgos, you were small but you remember Sakis' baba, right?'

Yorgos pauses his conversation with Jules.

'I remember him being a mountain! His big hands would take hold of mine and he would encourage me to walk up his legs, over his stomach, onto his chest, climb up him using my feet as he held my hand. Up and over his broad shoulders and sliding like a snake, down his back until I could reach his hand through his legs and I would tuck myself up tight and he would pull me through his legs. The game was not to touch the floor. Once round and then he would throw us up in the air like a ball. He did that to you too, eh Sakis?' He lifts his glass.

Sakis nods, raises his glass in return. He is doing his best to say as little as possible, save his throat.

'So, my boy.' Thanasis takes centre stage. The smell of roasting meat drifts amongst them, salads have been cut and put on the table along with piles of plates and forks. A woman is putting a tea towel over a big dish of feta to keep the flies off and a dog is sitting by a table leg, licking his lips, looking up hopefully. 'What brings you to breaking into your own house?'

A rumble heralds the school bus, noses press against the windows as the children inside spot the unexpected gathering of people. The bus drives past the house and stops in the village square further along. Within a minute, the schoolchildren begin to mix into the gathering. Hands reach for hunks of bread and slip under the tea towel for feta. A sea of black olives in a deep dish in the centre of the table drops a level and pits are thrown over the wall into Sakis' *yiayia's* overgrown garden. More glasses are brought and the water jug is refilled. Jugs of local wine cluster round an ouzo bottle on a separate table.

His neighbour is waiting for an answer. Why was he breaking into his own house?

It is a tricky question. If he tells them he has nowhere to live, he knows these people are so kind that he will get a dozen offers of a bed for the night. He would be grateful, of course, but somehow that would seal his role as the son of Costas the crocodile killer and, no matter how nice these people are, how kind and generous their natures, he is just not willing to do that. He has worked too hard to break free and prove himself on his own terms. Not one person has mentioned the competition that he won, not just for himself, but for his country. For all he knows, they may not even recognise him from the television. Maybe they didn't even watch it?

'I am just passing. Thought I would take a look,' he says vaguely. It's almost true, but an idea is beginning to form in a little corner of his heart. What about doing up the cottage as a little country escape, a place to retreat to if America gets too much? The melody that sifted through his soul earlier plays again in his heart, softer this time, not so aggressive, with a slower beat and the phrase end comes, too. He must play it as soon as he gets back to the hotel, remember the shapes of the chords in the patterns of his fingers.

'You not stopping then?' Dora asks, her eyes moistening as if her emotions live close to the surface. Over on his left, he can feel Jules staring at him.

'Well, it depends on what the inside is like. If it is not too bad, maybe I will stay a night.' There is no need to explain more to these people

'The inside will be fine,' Thanasis assures him. 'The roof developed a leak last winter, but I fixed that. Dora gives the place a sweep out every few months.'

'But there are no mattresses,' Dora interrupts. 'We had to throw them out years ago. I have some of the linen still, though. I hope you don't mind, but we have been using it. After you did not come for first one year and then two, it seemed the best thing to do.' She is fidgeting and her cheeks are red, as if she feels she has done something wrong.

'Good for you.' Sakis puts her at her ease.

'But why not stay with us?' Dora's face brightens.

'That is so kind,' Sakis says and Jules breaks away from Yorgos and comes to stand by his side. 'But I think I would prefer to revisit my *yiayia's* house.'

'I have a mattress you can have,' bird-like Anna offers. 'Then if you come again, it is all waiting for you.' Sakis smiles his thank you; Jules takes a step closer to him. 'Katerina, what happened to that one your brother gave to you? I thought you said it was in your way.'

'It is rolled up and in the *apothiki*.' She speaks as though irritated. Then her eyebrows raise and her face brightens. 'Ah, but you can come across and get it.' It is clear she would enjoy the process. She looks around the company, nodding and smiling at her own importance.

'Meat's done,' Yorgos announces, and this prompts everyone to take a plate. There is noise of cutlery and crockery. The patient dog barks and someone tells him to *Shh*. A child offers the animal a small piece of bread, which it sniffs at disinterestedly.

The more the villagers talk, the less his baba is mentioned, but nor does he get to assert himself and brag about his recent win. There is a moment when Katerina slips up beside him and whispers, 'I think everyone else was watching the *Olympiakos* match on the other side. You were very good. Well done.'

He turns to thank her and she smiles shyly.

'I think your friend Yorgos is the only person here who speaks English,' Jules interrupts them and Katerina looks down to her empty plate and heads toward the food. Jules has a plate of food piled so high that if he eats it all, he will not be hungry for months. Most of the people have gravitated to the table in the shade by the side of the house to sit and eat. The day is growing hot. The dog has taken refuge under the table and chickens strut from the backyard to clean up as crumbs are dropped. They show no fear.

As bellies fill, the chatter quietens. Thanasis and Yorgos pop over to Anna's for her mattress and then, to the disappointment of Katerina, they go and help her to retrieve a somewhat old and stained mattress from her *apothiki*. A key to the front door of Sakis' *yiayia's* cottage is found and, by the sound of things—unseen from where he is being persuaded to eat some more grilled chicken by Dora—the back door is force opened from the inside.

Sakis feels a strange excitement with the anticipation of seeing the inside of his childhood home again. Thanasis calls him over, but he does not want to go in with everyone there. He would prefer a quiet moment to allow the memories to flood back, so he cheerfully raises his glass and continues to talk to Dora, who says she will sort out enough bedding for them both. She also has some eggs he can take over; the chickens laid well today. She has a can of gas for the tiny camping gas stove that she knows his *yiayia* used to make her coffee on.

'It is lovely to have you home,' she says and her eyes grow moist again.

The day is getting hotter and the neighbours head for their homes, to sleep through the warmest part of the day. Katerina wishes Sakis a fond farewell.

'I remember you as a boy. You've not changed much,' she says and pats his hand in a way that reminds him of being that small boy all over again.

Thanasis says he must go and make sure his donkeys have enough water to drink, and Dora hands Sakis a bag full of sheets that smell freshly laundered. Jules is sitting at the table, picking through the remains of the food.

'I am going back over.' Sakis raises his eyebrows in the direction of the cottage. Jules pushes his chair back and stands.

Yiayia's **Cottage**

Sakis looks around. It is not another hotel, and definitely not his flat in Athens. It is just a room, sparse and plain. A chair by the bed, hooks on the back of the door where his clothes hang, and slithers of light slashing their way through the tightly fastened shutters. A glint on the wall, the gold of an icon, and he is grounded. *Yiayia's* house. A gecko runs zigzag up the wall by the door. A tendril of vine has found its way into the room through the shutters. He slept in this room when he was a boy. There is no rag rug on the floor by his bed as there was then, but otherwise nothing has changed. Well, there is precious little that could have changed. Four walls and a door!

He stretches and puts his hands behind his head. Yesterday, coming into the house after the impromptu gathering was a bit eerie. Mostly because he could not imagine the house inside without *Yiayia* being there, or the smell of her cooking and incense, or the bundles of sewing she always seemed to be doing. Even so, right from the creaking sound of the back door, it was all so familiar.

The small out room just inside the back door was empty. He couldn't even remember what *Yiayia* used to keep there. Newspapers perhaps, baskets and empty crates that the local farmers used for oranges. Oh yes, and the sheets she used to spread under the walnut tree, and under the edge of these were his Sunday shoes that rubbed his toes, and her big black waterproof boots for the winter, so big that if he held onto the doorframe, he could get both feet into one of them when he was small.

The handle on the door to the main room is just as he remembers it: black and shiny. It even feels the same, too: smooth and cold. Cautiously, he pulls the inner door open a crack, almost afraid of what he might find. A nervousness that the stored-away, time-faded images he cherishes as preserves of his life with *Yiayia* might be proved fake. Looking into the stillness beyond, he almost expects *Yiayia* to be there, her hair falling from its loose bun, her saggy black trousers wrinkling around her ankles under her greying skirt. She always seemed to wear so many clothes, even in summer. But of course she is not there. No extended arm invites him for a hug, no smells of the food she was forever cooking, just stillness.

The shutters, now half-open on either side of the glass-panelled front door, allow in some light. Amazingly, the net curtains over windows and door are still there, a little torn, sagging low, but still there. They diffuse what little sunlight sneaks its way in, a misty half-light that only illuminates the top surfaces of the furniture. The table in the middle of the room is still there, its surface white with dust, dully reflecting the light. The chairs on the side nearest to him are only visible as silhouettes against it. This is the table where his meals were eaten, games played, where *Yiayia* would lay out material to cut before she sewed. A gash of light on the left-hand wall glances off the glass of an icon that has hung there all his life, the image obscured by dust and reflection. On the opposite wall, the mirror is smoked with a fine layer of time. It was always too high for him to see himself in. Now it seems to be hung low. The wooden ceiling glows almost orange above his head and hanging in its centre like a black spider is the outline of *Yiayia's* mama's brass chandelier.

The room brings a flood of memories he didn't even know he had. Memories of games played on the marble-chip floor with Yorgos. The time he helped carry wood into the house and a log end had gone through one of the small green panes of glass in the front door.

It is strange letting all these thoughts flood back to him; things he has buried away, boxed up and stored hidden for all these years. Of all the feelings and emotional memories that crowd his senses, the most dominant one is a feeling of being loved. Not just by his *yiayia* but by the people of the village.

As he lies in his bed now, new pieces of history drift back to him. Katerina, the bird woman from across the road, talking with *Yiayia* in the doorway of his bedroom before coming in and sponging his forehead with a damp cloth. He must have had a fever. His mattress on the floor and Thanasis weaving rope across his bed frame, being allowed to help. He felt so grown up helping Thanasis.

'You awake?' Jules calls from the main room.

'Yes.' Harris and Eleftheria mew in their carrier. That, too, was a jolt, going from the faded past of the cottage to the shiny interior of the hotel to get them. Like two different lives, the old ways and the new ways. He knows which he prefers.

'You want coffee?'

'Thanks.'

'I'm going with Yorgos into Saros. There is a market on. You coming?'

'No.' He needs time to wake up. His throat is much better today. He is going to be fine for America, he can feel it, and Harris and Eleftheria are going to be happier here than in his old flat in Athens. Dora will feed them and they can roam in the garden freely and hunt for mice and beetles. Yes, he is definitely going to do the place up.

Jules returns laden with bags of shopping. Even though he knows Jules had no money, Sakis is somehow not surprised that he has acquired food.

'Do we owe Yorgos?' Sakis has being going through a chest of old papers, finding photographs of his *Papous* and *Yiayia* and of himself, in shorts, barefoot, smiling. There is a picture of his *yiayia* and his mama together, which creates a lump in his throat.

'No,' Jules says but offers no more. 'Is there no kitchen?'

Sakis looks up from a drawing with his name on it and his age, four, and points to the domed adobe oven with a stoke hole underneath and the worn stone counter next to it with two circular holes above a pair of arched stoke holes

87

below. Yiayia's cast iron soup pan still sits over one of the holes.

'You're kidding me?' Jules exclaims.

Now that he considers it, perhaps Jules has a point. They will have to get a fire going and wait for the embers to settle before they can even think of cooking. *Yiayia's* life must have been so hard. The melody that has been haunting him comes again and this time, he takes out his bouzouki and strums it through, adding bass notes and grace notes to add richness. At this stage, he normally has lyrics springing to mind, but this tune seems to be without words.

'That's nice.'

'It's new, but the words are not coming.'

'They will come.' Jules goes outside again as Sakis continues to work on the piece. It is nearly complete but still without words when he looks up again. His other senses have come back to life now the melody has a life of its own and will not be forgotten. The first sense to awaken is that of smell, and the most delicious aroma filling the room makes him realise he is hungry. Jules is standing by a metal countertop oven with an extension lead snaking out of the back door. His ability to gather for his needs is unbelievable.

'Ready in half an hour.' Jules goes outside again and soon returns, this time with a handful of something green, which he rubs between his palms over the cooking pot.

'You know, Jules, I am thinking of doing this place up, having it as a retreat for when America gets too much for us. What do you think?'

'I think it is *nécessaire*,' Jules says enthusiastically.

'So, seeing as you are here proving yourself to be the better cook, perhaps you could design the kitchen, the best layout?'

They take the food into the garden and sit beneath the walnut tree to eat at a rickety outdoor table.

'We have a day or two. We could start work now.' Jules' face is stippled in sunlight. The cicadas are rasping their love songs all around them in the orange trees and the chickens from Thanasis and Dora's houses have come over to scratch the earth around the table for scraps. The ground under the walnut tree is fairly clear but elsewhere, the garden is a knot of brown, crispy weeds. Cat-sized tunnels have been carved into this undergrowth, and smaller runs, maybe for rats or voles, criss-cross in between.

They talk of how the kitchen would be best laid out, the improvements that they could make elsewhere. The outside bathroom needs to be made integral, tiled, with a new suite. Sakis is amazed at how well they seem to agree on everything, and time spins away. A cat comes and sits on Jules' knee and at one point, one of the chickens even jumps on the table, and they laugh as they flap their arms to shoo it away.

The temperature builds and they retreat indoors, and air-conditioning is added to the list of improvements. They sleep away the afternoon and Sakis awakes in the evening feeling almost one hundred percent better.

'I'll go and find a phone and give Andreas a call,' he tell Jules, who is lying on the day bed in the main room. His clothes are hung over the carved wooden back and the curved armrests at either end.

'Ah, you are better. Brilliant! Listen, the whole disappearing act is working really well. They are offering just about anything they can to get an interview. If you come up at the beginning of next week, I will arrange an interview with Ant 1 television and I will choose a newspaper. The one that offers the most.' He laughs. 'Then you can fly immediately afterwards to America, give the impression that you are a big international star and that they should be pleased to get whatever time they can with you.' He laughs again.

'So do you have the tickets to America?' Sakis asks. Part of him does not want to wait to go back to Athens, instead to go now, immediately. His win seems so far away now, it might as well have never been. He wants to go to the city and pull back the thrill he felt in winning, the taste of success. But the thought of the reality of what waits for him in the city—the parties, the false friends, the glitz and the glamour—don't seem as attractive as they did when he was in the Ukraine, before he was ill.

'The tickets. Yes. Well, when I say yes, I mean almost. Just ironing out the last details.'

'Do we have any money yet?'

'Yes. I have put some in your account. Are you still in the hotel?'

'You told me to move out.' Sakis looks at the receiver as if this would explain Andreas' question.

'Ah yes, just a minor glitch. Well, you can move back now if you want. Live like a king till you come up to Athens. I'll send a car in a two or three days. Meanwhile, stay low, as your disappearance is really causing a stir. It is a stroke of genius.' He sounds very pleased with himself.

'It wasn't genius, Andreas. It was laryngitis,' Sakis reminds him.

'Yes, well you are better now, right? So all good. Stay low. If you are not at the hotel, where can I reach you?'

'If there is money in my bank, I will go and buy a mobile. Did you find my old one?'

'What, in all that chaos of parties in Kharkiv? Text me when you have one. Then we can be in touch. Bye.'

Sakis replaces the phone on the shelf of the kiosk in the village square and pays the lady who sits inside, surrounded by a plethora of everyday items that must be in constant demand. Cigarettes push for space next to batteries and boxes of paracetomol and bags of balloons hanging from a plastic strip. As she reaches for his coins, her sleeve knocks over a tray of insect repellent sprays, and these in turn send a pile of papers scattering to the floor around her feet.

'My accounts,' she says, giggling in a girlish way that is in contrast with her perfectly set hair and the crow's feet around her eyes. 'I hate them.' And as if to reinforce this statement, she makes no effort to pick up the fallen documents. Instead, she offers Sakis a wrapped sweet from a bowl on the counter, smiles warmly, and wishes him a good day.

Somewhere in the hills, the sound of goat bells echoes and another recollection overtakes him. He was alone, sent out by *Yiayia* to buy matches, the box tightly gripped in his hand. The square was filling with sheep and goats as they were herded home, the biggest goats taller than him. They had seemed too big. Their underbellies hung with droppings and mud, the hooves clicking on the road, the animals' beards making them somehow human. He had been scared. Their slit eyes upon him, some of them so tall they looked down at him as they came. They trotted with speed; he was afraid. He had muffled his scream. Then arms were around him. He was lifted off his feet and then he was inside the kiosk. It smelt of perfume and hairspray and he was offered a sweet in a wrapper.

Sakis turns to look at the kiosk lady again. Surely it could not be the same person? Has she sat here all these years, doing the same job, meeting the same people? She smiles and waves again.

She had given him such comfort back then. Told him that she was afraid and how kind it was of him to stay with her until the animals had gone. He had left the kiosk walking tall. A man who had protected someone.

Renovating the Cottage.

With some money in the bank and the promise of more on the way, Sakis and Jules decide to start work immediately on the cottage. With all the shutters open, the sun streams into the cottage, highlighting charm—and age. At the very least, everywhere needs a coat of paint but if they are seriously going to spend any time here, it needs more.

It is not a hard decision to go in to Saros to look at plans for kitchens. The kitchen salesman's brother is an architect, so they drift from one establishment to another to enquire about an extension. Jules has ideas of how the cooking area will work best and they both agree with the architect that a utility room for a washing machine should also be added.

The creativity of what they are doing is fun but Sakis feels out of his depth and consequently very reliant on Jules. When he finally got his own flat in Athens, it was fully finished. Before that, in his struggle to make enough for his own place, he always lived in other peoples' houses as a lodger, a sofa surfer. Nowhere was ever permanent. It was always a struggle.

Playing sweaty smoke-filled nightclubs—and often conned out of his earnings—but with each club a little better than the last until after ten hard years, Andreas spotted him. Even Andreas was amazed that it did not happen earlier, as his talent was always recognisable.

Well, it was recognised: the nightclub owners saw it, the wheelers and dealers saw it. The truth was everyone wanted a piece, and that left very little for him. But Andreas really seemed to want to represent him and with that representation and the connections Andreas had, he was suddenly in demand at the larger bouzouki clubs in Athens. His face filled billboards around where he worked until Andreas made his cheeky, and, perhaps a little premature, move of putting him up against big names to represent Greece in the competition.

Sakis watches Jules taking the pencil from the architect to draw lines on the rough sketch they are working on together, which it seems he cannot describe without a common language. The architect is smiling, approving of the suggestion. Jules seems so comfortable in any situation, completely at ease with whoever he talks to. Sakis is very lucky to have found him as a friend. Just in his company, Sakis can feel himself unwind, not hold so tight to life, generally panic less.

In all those years of communal living and hand-to-mouth existence, he never made a real friend. Not really, unless you count Andreas. There were people who pretended to be his friend but really, it always turned out that their motives were selfish and ulterior. That singer, for example, who was trying for a quick leg up the nightclub rankings using his musical talent— and stealing some of his songs in the process. Or the time when he was pushed into being a frontman for a group because of his face, not his talent, and then dropped in favour of a girl's face when the moment suited.

So to now be surrounded by a village of people who genuinely seem to wish him well and to have Jules by his side is unnerving and alien. Part of him would like to thank Jules for being his friend, but how can he put that into words? Besides, it would feel awkward to tell Jules how much he appreciates his support, his care when he was ill, his companionship whilst he waits to go to New York. Sure, Jules has asked for a bit of help once they are there, but he would want to do everything he can for Jules after the friendship he has shown.

And now this! This planning to renovate the cottage so they have somewhere to return to when New York becomes overbearing. The organising of the rooms so they can both live there comfortably.

It is remarkable how quickly the ideas become decisions. An extension is to be built to house both utility room, kitchen, new bathroom, and second bedroom. The traditional oven is to be left as a feature in the main room. Oil fired central heating is to be installed. The chimney to the fireplace needs raising apparently, to stop the backdraft of smoke that Sakis can remember used to give him a sore throat in the winters. The window in the bedroom is to be replaced with double doors into the garden and the garden—well, that can wait a while, but there is talk of digging out an area that will later be paved and covered with a vine-adorned pergola. That work might as well be done when they dig the foundations for the extension. Maybe they will even put a water feature somewhere, or a swimming pool beyond the walnut tree, in amongst the orange trees.

Sakis cannot remember feeling this happy—except when singing.

Then he always is this happy.

The architect makes a call and workers are scheduled in. 'Strictly speaking, we should wait for the planning permission to be issued,' he says with a smile, 'but there in the village, no one will object, and it is really just a formality…' They can start the work whilst he and Jules are away.

'Next summer, we can come for a holiday and it will all be done!' Sakis enthuses later that evening. Taking his bouzouki by its neck, he strolls to the far end of the garden, through the weeds that will be dug up, to sit on the low wall that will be repaired, and there he plays out his new melody. It is a full and haunting tune now, complete.

'That's beautiful,' Jules says when he returns to the house.

'But the words don't come,' Sakis mourns. 'I don't even know what it should be about.' It annoys him that he seems to have such a block.

'They'll come,' Jules says and pours them both an ouzo. The night settles in. An orange glow bleeds from behind the shutters at the back of Thanasis and Dora's house, lending high contrast to the scattering of geraniums in brightly painted olive oil tins around the back door. Across the road, Katerina pulls her shutters closed. Next door to her, Anna's house is already closed for the night, and a hum of television sounds leaches into the stillness. The smell of jasmine is on the breeze and the village dogs are barking their evening chorus. Now and again as the wind direction changes, the jasmine is replaced with the smell of orange blossom. They are the smells of his childhood.

Somewhere up the street, someone is laughing. It is probably coming from the eatery near the square, with tables and chairs arranged on the pavement, around a tree that someone has wrapped up with fairy lights—a crude village attempt at enticement.

If only the owners knew that it is not the magical glow of the fairy lights that draws people, or him at least, but rather the familiarity that these villagers offer to both family and stranger. An unspoken acknowledgement that everyone is human and therefore equal. His competition win does not matter here; his transient fame bears no consequence on the present. Here, all that seems to matter is the moment. The conversation at hand, the immediate surroundings, the person in front of you.

It was his home once, so it should not surprise to him that here he has the feeling of coming home. But it does surprise him. What really rattles him is that, only by being here and feeling part of the village, he realises he has yearned for this for years. In his striving ever forward to some future situation where he would be surrounded by 'better' musicians, 'better' nightclubs, 'better' wages, 'better' friends, it was all just a thin veneer that, if he had picked at its surface, would have revealed that the real hunger was to belong somewhere.

In this village, he belongs. With Jules, he belongs. Maybe Jules is the brother he never had? The father, mother, and friend he never had.

'What if we decide not to go to New York? What if we decide to stay here?' Sakis says, pouring a second ouzo and then lighting a citronella candle. The mosquitoes are out in force tonight.

'What if?' Jules returns the question.

'Well, would you be so sorry? Does this place not make you happy?'

'It is a very happy place. The cottage is very peaceful; you seem content here.' Jules stretches out in one of the new directors chairs they brought home earlier. He always melts into wherever he sits, but this chair seems to really suit his posture.

'Could you live here? Permanently? I could get a job in a local club, or maybe even teach music to the local children.' Sakis plays with the idea.

'Could be very good.' Jules does not seem to be really entering the conversation. He is looking up at the stars. With so few street lights anywhere in the village and no lights at all in the surrounding countryside, the sky is black and the stars wink one behind the other, layer after layer, further and further away in the warm night sky. Somewhere in the village, someone plays a traditional tune on the clarinet. A cat slinks out of the dried weeds, walks with such confidence right up to them, and then jumps on Jules' lap. Jules doesn't stop gazing up at the night sky, but he strokes the stray absentmindedly.

'The day after tomorrow is the village saint's day,' he says.

'The *panigyri*? Oh. What made you think of that?'

'Can you not hear someone practising? Are you going to sing for them?'

The next day, they are raised from sleep by a persistent knocking on the front door. Two quality mattresses are delivered along with the new bed linen, towels, and net curtains they ordered. As they surface from sleep and take the items, something seems unusual. The delivery man waves a cheerful goodbye and it is only when he has driven off that they become properly aware of the activity in the street. People are armed with thick, floppy brushes, and everything is getting a coat of whitewash. The clarinettist is now in competition with several guitars and at least two sources of recorded music. Up towards the square, the activity increases. Chairs are being unloaded from a lorry, a stage has been erected, the kiosk is strung with Greek flags around the edges of its roof. Sakis hovers, enjoying the feeling of excitement. Some children run from a house further down up towards the square, screaming to each other, pushing, smiling, hair flowing behind the girls, little jumps as their *kefi* overflows.

'*Kalimera*,' Thanasis calls as he straightens up stiffly from the other side of his front door, whitewash brush dripping. 'Done yours.' He flicks the brush toward Sakis' wall. 'But your whole place could do with a lick, eh? Are you looking forward to the *panigyri*? It has been a while since you have been here for one. Should be a good one this year. We have booked

Grigoris Taxydaktylos from Thessaloniki to come down to sing. His ancestors are from these parts, you know.'

'I can't say I've heard of him.'

'No, well, he is an old guy. Mainly does village *panigyria*. But they say he is a great talent.'

'Well, to be honest I might not see. I might …'

But his sentence is cut off.

'What! Oh you must. It is once a year! Don't tell me you do not remember how much fun you used to have at the *panigyria*?

Sakis does remember. He remembers the games of chase with the other children in and around the tables and chairs that filled the village square and all the people that came from Saros, different from the villagers somehow: crisper, shinier. To one side of the square on the road, they built a huge fire and roasted pig after pig, tray after tray pulled from the embers and carved on the spot. Barrels of ice were everywhere, filled with bottles of beer, ouzo at every table, everyone in their finest. The streets down in front of the house filled with trestle tables, piled with treasures for sale—trinkets for the children and work tools for the farmers. *Yiayia* would haggle for a new pruning saw every year. The last year he can remember, there was someone selling air rifles for the boys and guns for those who like to hunt rabbits. How he had wanted one of those!

'Well, it is just …'

'Sakis, I think the mattress is the wrong size. Can you get the man with the van back?'

With a shrug as if to say 'what can I do?' Sakis abandons his conversation with Thanasis and goes inside.

'Ah, no, it probably just needs a good shove.' Sakis pulls off blankets and pillow and with a shove and a push, the mattress fits perfectly.

'I should hear from Andreas today about the tickets to America. He is also going to set up a couple of interviews in Greece before we go.'

Jules, who is taking sheets out of their paper wrappings, looks up.

'Should I wait before I make the bed up, then? Is it definite that you are going?'

'Yes. Well, sort of. Andreas sounded sure, but nothing is sure until it is done, right?' He picks up his bouzouki. A new melody has come to mind, a few notes that will fit in the middle of the tune. He works the riff for a moment before playing the new song he wrote. Maybe the words will come today?

'That is my favourite,' Jules says.

A knock at the open front door is accompanied by a cheerful voice.

'Yeia sas.' Sakis covers his surprise at seeing the owner of the hotel at his door. Jules shows no sign of being shocked.

'Stella,' she reminds him. 'And this,' she steps inside and behind her is a younger woman, not much more than a girl, 'is Abby, an English friend of mine, here for the *panigyri.*' Between the two of them, they carry a long, rolled-up rug. But Sakis cannot take his gaze from Abby. She has such strength in her features, yet she is as delicate as a poppy.

'Hello.' Sakis reverts to English to wish Abby welcome.

'I heard you were doing up the place and I wondered if you needed a rug? I know it is summer now, but when winter comes, these stone floors can get very cold.' Stella speaks in her native Greek.

'How kind of you,' Sakis says in English. He does not want to exclude this Abby person from their conversation.

'It is new. It was in the hotel when I bought it but it is not the right style. Oh my, it is hard to believe that this place has not been lived in for fifteen years,' Stella says as Sakis takes the back end of the rolled rug from Abby. Jules grabs the front end.

'Dora has kept it well over the years,' Sakis says and, looking at Abby, he adds, 'People are very nice around here.'

'You will be at the *panigyri* tomorrow night?' Stella asks, but it sounds more like a statement than a question.

'You are going?' Sakis asks Abby.

'I came over especially, that and a little business with Stella.' Abby's voice is so English, it makes his stomach tremor.

'Right. Plenty to do.' Stella looks distracted for a moment, as if consulting an internal list of things to be accomplished. 'Let me know if I can be of help?' before leading the way back out into the sunshine.

'See you at the *panigyri*,' Sakis calls after Abby, who turns and smiles at the garden gate.

'Ha! You have just been struck by lightning, my friend.' Jules laughs when the two women are out of earshot.

'I have not.' Sakis watches the figures as they recede into the square and are lost in the beehive of activity.

Jules laughs again. 'Sure,' he agrees as he gathers things together to make breakfast.

Jules pushes his plate away and sips his second coffee. They have taken a table round to the front of the house so they can watch as stalls are erected and people hurry about. The sound of laughter seems to be contagious across the whole village. There is a little shouting here and there, as if the excitement has turned to tension and has bubbled over. A massive stack of amplifiers is unloaded from a truck, and they stand marooned in the middle of the road.

More neighbours are out whitewashing. The walls that were painted earlier have dried from a dull grey to a startling white.

The woman from the kiosk is striding down the road at a brisk pace. It seems odd to see her with legs; normally, all that can be seen of her is her head and shoulders. She is carrying a heavy-looking paper bag with handles. Much to Sakis' surprise, she stops before reaching his gate and beckons him.

'*Ella edo.*' She demands him to *come here*. Sakis naturally looks about to see if it is really him she is talking to. '*Ella* Sakis,' she says again, out of breath with the speed of her walk and the weight of the bag. Sakis stands and realises he ate too much breakfast, but then, Jules is such a good cook. This morning, he rubbed garlic and tomatoes on the toast before piling the slices with scrambled egg.

'Can I help you, er …' Did he ever know her name, this woman who saved him from the sheep all those years ago?

'Vasso,' she says. 'I heard you were moving in. They may be no good, but I was having a clear out, always do for the *panigyri*, clear out and whitewash.' She laughs as if this is funny. 'Found these curtains. If they are no good, give them to the gypsies. Oh, and Marina who runs the corner shop says she has some household things that you might find useful. Just pass by. See you tomorrow night if not before.' She doesn't wait for a reply but pats him on the shoulder and rushes back the way she came.

Sakis experiences a wave of guilt. Everyone's kindness is so touching. They must think he is staying permanently.

The bag is heavy. Once back by Jules, he sits and pulls out a corner of the material. They are fully lined blackout curtains in blue velvet. One edge is faded by the sun.

'Cool,' Jules says. 'You know, they call this shabby-chic. I like it.'

'Bedroom or main room, then? Or yet-to-be-built bedroom?' He loves the way Jules is so positive about everything, even a pair of old curtains.

There is a ringing from inside. Sakis almost knocks the table over as he jumps up to get it. It will be Andreas. His future is about to begin.

It isn't Andreas. It is a wrong number. But now that he is up, he might as well call Andreas. Otherwise he will just be waiting. He goes out the back door, down to the walnut tree, and leans against its trunk to dial.

'Hi, Andreas?'

'Who is this?'

'Sakis!'

'Ah Sakis, I did not recognise your number. Of course, you have a new phone.'

Sakis is about to remind Andreas that he texted his new number but he wants to get to the point.

'Have you got them?'

'Got what?'

'Andreas, are you teasing me? Don't, please. I have been sitting here waiting. When do we go to America? When shall I come up to Athens?'

'Ahhh, yes, okay. Well, there has been just the tiniest hitch…'

Sakis' head jerks back. He stares into the middle distance but sees nothing. The sun loses some of its warmth and his legs feel weak.

'What? Come on! You said that you were trying to get them to pay. If they won't, they won't, so you get the tickets yes? You have set things up the other end, right? So we must go.'

'Sakis, life is not as easy as that. There are complications. There is this model, Naomi. She is big, huge! She is coming to Greece just for a couple of days and she needs a local man, like me, to pave the way, show her which doors to go through, and open a few doors, too.'

'Andreas, you are meant to be my manager!' He slithers down the tree to crouch on the ground.

'I am, I am. This gig with this Naomi, it will pay for the tickets to America. You'll see; it will all come together.'

'And the interviews you had lined up for me in Athens?'

'Well, I have been a bit busy organising this visit of Naomi's. The television want to interview her; the press want to talk to her.'

Suddenly it is clear that it has gone! His moment that he should have grabbed has passed him by! He is yesterday's news. Unromantically, a bout of laryngitis has stolen his chance. He should never have trusted Andreas.

'Sakis? You still there?'

'Yes.' His tone is flat. He has no energy even to argue; what would be the point?

'Two days. Then she'll be gone and I can buy the tickets. Trust me, Sakis. Just two days?'

He does not even bother to reply. He ends the call, uses the tree to help him stand and, stiff legged, rejoins Jules.

'Was it him?' he asks. Sakis cannot reply. 'Hey, you okay? You look pale. What's happened?'

'It's gone. My chance has gone. That bloody Andreas. No tickets, no America. Gone.' His head hangs so low, the back of his neck hurts, but he does not care.

'No, man! You still won.'

'There are no tickets, no money, and nothing lined up.'

'But you still won. People will still want to interview you. Buy your own ticket. Sort it out yourself.'

Sakis shakes his head.

'Why do you shake your head? If you want it, do it. It is like everything in life. If you want something, the only person who is going to make it happen is you. If you wait for someone else to give it to you, you will wait forever.'

'I don't have his contacts, his experience.'

'Yet,' Jules says.

'What?'

'You don't have his contacts and his experience yet. But if you want it, you can get it.'

Sakis watches an ant carrying a crumb of scrambled egg twice its size.

'I hear you,' he says but he does not feel any lighter.

'Maybe you need to know what you want,' Jules suggests.

Sakis goes inside and takes his bouzouki to his room. He has not sung since the laryngitis but now he needs to sing, quietly, to himself. He plays his new song, but still the words do not come. It is the most beautiful, passionate tune he has ever written. But the words do not come. He resorts to singing some old tunes. He is almost tempted to sing and play 'Opa' but he knows now, he knows now so strongly, it was a sell-out. A cheap ditty to get him in the competition. Maybe he does not want to go down the road that winning with such a song set before him. Maybe it will lead to more sell-outs, more cheap tricks, more soulless singsongs.

The day moves by him with no effort on his behalf. The village is transformed, with the road cordoned off to traffic as more and more market stalls are erected and flags are strung wherever there is a place to string them. He spends most of the day in the bedroom, which is naturally cool as the walls are stone and over half a meter thick.

Jules leaves him alone, tapping on the door to bring him a sandwich at lunchtime and again in the evening to invite him for food.

'Figured out what you want?' Jules asks as he serves up a mixed salad. He has also made a dish of *tzatziki* and *dolmades* using cabbage leaves.

Sakis doesn't answer. They eat in silence. They drink ouzo in silence. Finally, Jules yawns noisily and says, 'I heard three new tunes today. That's a productive day.'

'The words won't come,' Sakis replies.

'Maybe the words that you think should come are not the right ones. Maybe you are waiting for the wrong inspiration.'

'I sing of passion, I sing of the old ways, I sing of how proud Greece should be. I sing the songs of the *manga* of Pireaus.'

'Yes, you did,' Jules says and Sakis downs the rest of his ouzo as he hears the past tense, and goes to bed.

The Panigyri

Sakis wakes with such joy the next day. There is no accounting for it, no reason. He is just happy. As for New York or Andreas, he has no appetite for thinking about such things. Maybe he will ponder over it all, but right now, the whole things feels too negative. Energy for no purpose.

The sun creeps through the shutters and a chorus of birds are singing. He stretches and creaks back a wooden shutter, a blade of light cutting through the sitting room's still air to slice across Jules' ruffled empty bed.

Sakis finds him sitting outside at the back, looking across the overgrown garden. The skin on his forehead is creased and his mouth is tightened in a thin line.

'Your mattress too hard?' Sakis asks as he pours himself a coffee and then leaves it on the table as he picks up his bouzouki to strum a chord or two. He breaks into one of the new melodies from yesterday, which morphs into the haunting tune that he is most happy with. But still, the words for this tune will not come.

Jules has not spoken yet.

A rustling in the dried weeds promises the arrival of a cat, probably the one that seems to adore Jules. But no cat comes and the rustle continues until a tortoise appears.

'Can you see him?' Sakis asks Jules.

Jules still does not speak.

'Come on, Jules. So you miss this chance of being taken to New York and I am no longer the man who could open doors for you over there. But being here is not that bad. You said yourself we could be happy here. I will get work at some bouzouki bar. I will take on lessons for children. It may not be the big time, but I think we might find we fit in well here.' The words come of their own accord, taking Sakis by surprise, bringing a smile to his lips that expands to crease the corners of his eyes. His stomach flips in a leap of delight at his prospects.

But Jules' lips still remain a tight line.

They eat breakfast in silence, but even that does not shake Sakis' high spirits. After breakfast, he picks up his instrument again and continues to strum. New melodies leak into old, tiny riffs take on bigger forms. He watches his hands almost as if they are not part of him as inspiration after inspiration manifests. He feels caught on a wave of creativity, as melody after melody crescendos and falls away. It feels like there is no end to them, as if these notes have been waiting all this time just for him to come to this garden and find them so both the notes and Sakis can rise above the orange trees and fly on their wings.

Jules stands up so suddenly, his chair rocks. Without a word or a look, he goes inside and comes out again with his small rucksack. It is bulging.

'Ahh, yes, we need to get a washing machine,' Sakis says as he looks at the bag and continues to strum. Words are floating in his head. This tune is a sad ballad about people who remember once living in the city, where they behaved like the chickens, pecking and strutting but finding no corn. He keeps hold of the words in his mind as he speaks, 'We should have got one the other day. I don't suppose there will be a laundrette in the village. Are you going into Saros?'

'No. Athens.'

Sakis stops strumming.

'I have a plane to catch,' Jules adds.

Sakis puts down his instrument, worried he might drop it.

'A plane?' He hears the sound of his own voice. His throat tightens to laugh, but he is not sure if it is a joke.

'I have always had my ticket, Sakis.' The words are spoken softly, as an apology.

'To where?' Sakis breathes the words rather than speaking them.

'Come on man, you know. I want to work for *Underground Unchained*. Nothing has changed for me.'

'But …' Sakis looks around to the house, the area of ground that they marked out with sticks and stones where the extension will be.

'But what?' Jules' voice is gentle, his French accent strong. 'You knew from when we first met this was my dream, that I was going for it.'

'But the house. What was all this designing and planning with the house?' Although he is sitting down, he feels as if he is falling and a little bit dizzy, as if he has drunk too much coffee. His breakfast turns in his stomach, an empty gnawing sensation that leaves him feeling slightly sick.

Jules puts down his bag and pulls his chair up close to Sakis before he too sits down. With a hand on Sakis' shoulder, he looks him in the eyes.

'Sakis, my friend, my dear friend, the house, the kitchen, the extension, it was never for me. It was always for you.'

Sakis can feel his lower lip tremble.

'But you said it was, you used a French word, *nécessaire*.'

'This house, this village, it is very *nécessaire*. For you. This is what you need.' His voice softens even more. 'Not me.'

The world becomes blurred behind suspended tears. Jules drops his hand to his lap.

'Do not be sad, my friend. I think you are going to be happy here. As for me, I have to conquer my own mountain, win my own world competition. I still have things to prove. Maybe when I have worked for the magazine for a while, maybe I will come back here. You can never tell the future.'

But Sakis knows he will not come back.

Jules picks up his bag.

Sakis points to the house. The words Jules has spoken still have not landed, have yet to make their impact. He needs to hear them again. 'You did all this …'

'For you.' His hand is back on his shoulder. 'For you, my friend. You would never have been brave enough to even consider living in the village on your own. But now, you have a picture in your head of how the house will be, a picture of how life will be. Can you imagine living anywhere else now?'

'Thank you.' Sakis cannot trust himself to say any more. If he says anything else, he will lose control. His bottom lip is still trembling. He has never known such thoughtfulness, such selfless kindness. Jules pulls Sakis' head into the curve of his neck and rests his own forehead on Sakis' shoulder for a moment. Jules smells of soap and coffee and musty t-shirt. The house is going to be so empty without him.

Releasing his grip slightly, Jules lifts his head first and they face each other. Jules kisses him first on one cheek and then on his other, prolonging the release. There is real love in his kisses.

'*A bientôt, mon ami.*' Jules looks him in the eye and then abruptly stands, throws his bag over one shoulder, and he is gone, striding down the road toward the village square.

Sakis sits without moving, stunned, only breaking from his stare when the tortoise noisily chomps on a lettuce leaf that Jules must have put down for it. He falls into a stare, watching the tortoise take deliberate bites at the lettuce, until it is all gone and the animal moves off, slowly, slowly. The sounds from the village square leak into his ears only half heard.

'*Ena, duo, ena, do, ena ena, ena.*' The sound check repeats over and over, reminding the village that the festivities are tonight. The hum of generators as they are started to check that they will provide enough light for the stalls when it grows dark mingles with the sounds of tractors as, for the rest of the village, daily normal work continues.

'Ena, duo, ena.'

There is the smell of baking effusing from next door. Dora is making her prize-winning *spanakopita*. A donkey sucks in noisy air up on the hillside before bellowing it out again with all the sad loneliness that Sakis feels and thinks is going to break his aching heart. Jules has gone.

'Ah, there you are.' It is bird-like Katerina from the house opposite. 'I brought you some jam that I made last autumn, some pickles from the winter, a bottle of my homemade wine, and a bottle of oil from my olive grove to officially welcome you to the village.' She blushes. Sakis is roused and feels forced to respond.

'Oh, thank you. That is very kind. You really needn't have.' The words come parrot-fashion.

'Sakis.' She sits on Jules's chair. 'I, or rather we, the village, need a favour.'

This makes him blink.

'The *panigyri* was going to be so great this year. You know we had Grigoris Taxydaktylos from Thessaloniki booked. You know, Taxydaktylos, the singer and clarinettist? Grigoris?' Sakis looks blank but she continues anyway. 'Well, he just called. His car is broken down. Up near Larisa. He is not going to make it.' She waits for him to say something but when he doesn't, she continues. 'I know who you are. I know you are no longer Sakis the son of Costas. You are Sakis the winner of the song contest.'

Her words shock him and he realises he had forgotten. Extraordinary as that seems, he had really forgotten. In his sorrow of first losing the New York deal and then losing Jules, he has forgotten the feeling of his win. He has also forgotten being known as the son of Costas. The two emotions return and tussle, swamping his grief at finding himself alone.

Katerina has one hand shielding the sun from her eyes as she looks at him. The tortoise's nails tick tick across the flags as it makes its way into the undergrowth.

Sakis still says nothing.

'They don't know, the villagers. They don't know who you are. *Olympiakos* were playing against Spain the night you won … The whole village sat in the square watching the football.'

'So?' Sakis begins to see which way this is going. He is not sure he likes the direction, so he waits for her to spell it out as he tries to focus in on his own responses, trying to examine and name his emotions.

'So, you could be a surprise like the *panigyri* has never known. You, Sakis, could make this the best *panigyri* the village has ever known. You could make this so good that Saros town will never be able to better tonight. The competition between the town and the village will be over and the village will have won forever. They will never be able to better this because you are a local boy, not someone bought and shipped in. You are one of us! Can you imagine?' The pride shines in her eyes.

The confusion in his head is now fighting with a tremor in his chest.

'Please say you will do it. We won't tell anyone. I am the musical coordinator, so I will just say the problem is solved and then, pow! We will hit them between the eyes.' She makes a tiny movement with her fist that is meant to be a punch in the air.

The tremor in his chest is the one he always gets with the excitement of a live performance. The confusion in his head is trying to separate and name all the feelings that are racing through his heart, his veins, his mind.

'I, I, I ...' If he is to perform, he will need to practice. 'There are not enough hours.'

'For what? Just sing. I have seen you. Become lost in your world and you will take all those watching with you.'

'But ...' What would he sing? Not 'Opa.' He is never going to sing that crass little jingle again. He could sing some of his older songs, the ones about life in Pireaus but somehow, they no longer seem to fit who he is. They are too heavy for life here. He has nothing to sing!

'Please, Sakis.' She is so earnest in her entreaties, her eyes now screwed up against the sun because she has lowered her arm to hold his hand, her wrinkled digits on his smooth, tanned musical fingers.

Someone says 'yes' and she smiles. Sakis realises it is him. Again, he has agreed to something to please someone else. Does he really want to perform? The excitement he feels says 'yes' and Katerina releases her grip. The delight on her face mingles with the excitement now bubbling inside him and he is soaring. The optimism he felt from before Jules' departure returns with gusto.

'Yes, I would love to,' he repeats, and her smile becomes even wider.

'Not a word to anyone.' She is up on her feet, little bird-like steps as she hops towards her home.

Sakis spurts a half laugh out through his nose, his own smile turning into laughter. He chuckles to himself. Tonight, he will perform and take the world with him once again. But right now, he needs to practice. He must get some words together for his new tunes and hopefully words for that haunting tune. Surely they must come. Now is the time to let this most beautiful of melodies loose for other people to enjoy.

Light on his feet, he takes his bouzouki into his bedroom and the hours fly by as the words to his newest tunes come, lyrics follow more lyrics, but still after many hours, there are no words to the one haunting melody. It does not even have a title. He is slightly disappointed not to have that one tune to offer, but his others are good. Really good. In fact, he confides to himself, they are better than anything he has written for some time.

He stands in the shadows. The sun has gone. The moon is full but the stars are unseen as the lighting next to humming generators floods the square. On stage is a really talented old school zither player. Sakis is taken aback to find such passion, such sensitivity, understanding so far from the glitter of the Athens music clubs.

'He's good, isn't he?' Katerina whispers in his ear. 'He's got the farm down by the river.' Sakis turns to look at her to see if she is joking. Her face is shining as she watches the old man play.

Before the old man, there was another man who was very capable on the bouzouki. Not technically brilliant, but he created such a mood, such an intensity. And there was a woman with a voice like grinding stone and toffee who, when she sang, reached deep inside him, making her performance feel personal, exposing. He had blushed. She was mesmerising to watch. Maybe, all these years, he has been facing the wrong direction. Maybe he should have headed towards the fields, not the bright lights of Athens to find the most sincere performers.

'You're on.' Katerina takes to the stage first to introduce him.

'Ladies and gentlemen, I have a surprise. He is one of our own. He is here to play for you tonight. Sakis!'

A group of young girls at one table clap enthusiastically. Maybe they are fans of the song contest, or perhaps they have just drunk too much wine. As he steps onto the stage, there is a polite clapping from everyone, but he can also hear whispers of, 'Isn't that the son of Costas?' and a few giggles and references to the crocodile killer. He has to push himself to keep going onto the stage, the tremor in his chest now a sickness in his belly. Like every other time at this point, it would take very little to make him turn and run. Run and run until he is far away from the brutal exposure of singing his songs on stage.

He strums his fingers across his bouzouki strings to make sure he is in tune and settles himself comfortably. He strums once more and *tzing*, his D string snaps and curls up on itself. He has spares in his instrument case, but this could be his excuse to take his leave.

He slips from the stool and walks to the edge of the platform, wondering if the shake in his legs is visible. He could just put his instrument away now and keep walking. A movement in the crowd near the stage catches his eye. Abby straightens her skirt at the back to sit down next to Stella. She looks him right in the eyes and gives him a warm smile and a little nod as if to say 'go on.'

There is a compartment in the case where the strings are kept. His fingers tremble as he moves a piece of folded paper to get to the strings. The crowd talk amicably amongst themselves as he puts on the new string and stuffs the old broken string back into the compartment, then picks up the folded paper. He is about to stuff that in too when he wonders what it is.

Unfolding the sheet, he recognises Jules' handwriting. He reads. He reads again. The words blur with unspilt tears but also a smile comes to his lips. Standing with confidence, he flashes Abby his best smile, his head turned to the side so the slight overlap of his teeth doesn't show. Taking his place again on stage, instead of playing the tune he rehearsed in his bedroom, he opens with the chords of the haunting melody.

The square silences. Even the children in their best clothes and bows stop running between tables. The whole village is on hold and then come the words that Jules has left him, on a folded sheet tucked in his bouzouki case. The title is 'Amongst the Orange Trees'. The words fit

his haunting tune and enhance all its
exquisiteness.

He begins to sing and, for him, the world
disappears as nature closes in on him, the heat of
the day wraps over him, the cicadas become his
chorus, the olive trees sway to his melody, and
time stands still as the moment is captured.

> *'I didn't set my alarm last night*
> *I woke up this morning with the new sun*
> *gently warming my face.*
> *I got dressed*
> *I didn't put on my watch*
> *I told the time by the rumbles in my belly*
> *I dined on its silence all day*
> *I listened to myself for a change*
> *Outside I listened to the birds*
> *They didn't chastise me for*
> *my ignoring them for so long*
> *They were happy to have my ears back*
> *to listen to their song*
> *I was happy to listen*
> *I was lost without thought*
> *A deeper connection that leaves me vacant*
> *to not think*
> *and just be*
> *for that moment amongst the orange trees.*

There is a deadly hush as the song echoes its end and then, as a mass, the village is on its feet. The girls gathered at one table scream as if he is a pop star. The zither player, when their eyes meet, bows deeply. Katerina is hopping from one foot to the other, and Abby is clapping with her mouth open, eyes open, and hopefully her heart open.

It is as if he has won again. But this win is more than he ever hoped for. He has just won a place on the earth he can call home, and found music at his fingertips that is a real reflection of his spirit.

It seems almost a shame to spoil the moment with more music. But the village is waiting, and he does play on, and they accept each offering with greater applause than the last. But he knows the first was the best.

When he finally steps from the stage, Katerina is all of a dither.

'Did you see him?' she asks.

'Who?' Sakis has no real interest; his eyes are on Abby. Maybe he can sit with her, walk with her, dance with her.

'That big guy. What's his name from Athens Music,' she enthuses. But Sakis has no interest.

Stella welcomes him to her table and Abby's eyes are for him alone.

The next day, Sakis wakes slowly. Following Jules' advice, he did not set an alarm, and his watch is discarded by the bed. Over breakfast, the sun warms his face and the birds sing to him, whispering new tunes, peeping out their own lyrics.

But it is not to be a day of peace.

He leaves the hot pot of breakfast coffee to briefly wander to the kiosk in the square for a paper, only to discover that the local rags are full of the discovery of a 'new star'. Vasso, the lady in the kiosk, enthuses and praises his performance, but he insists he must return before his coffee is cold.

He turns to leave just as a local television crew turns up, and they insist that he be interviewed on the spot. Then the local radio network arrives and they encourage and pressure him to sing for Saros radio, live, there and then.

This completed, he finds an opportunity to sneak away, only to be halted by a national television van pulling up. Was he born here in the village, they want to know? Who influenced him as he grew up? Is he pleased that 'Opa' is the number one selling song in Greece for the fourth week running?

It is with considerable relief that he finds a moment to escape and, undetected, he runs home. As he hurries around to the back of the house, his phone rings, rasping the air. He stops by the back door to answer it.

'Hi, Sakis. Well, you did not waste any time, did you?' Andreas' voice sounds familiar but misplaced. It does not fit in the village any more. 'I don't suppose you have read the online version of *The Athens Musical Express*, have you?'

Sakis is about to answer when Andreas continues.

'It says that since winning, you have branched out in a new direction, and let me read this bit out to you: "A new direction that is as alive and as passionate as anything that has been heard in Greece for a long time. Sakis takes traditional Greek music to a new height where only a few will be able to accompany him".'

Sakis watches the tortoise and thinks about the coffee going cold. Does he have any more lettuce?

'There is also a piece in *Online Urban Unchained*. It's a good piece by Jules, but I am not sure you should have given him permission to publish the lyrics to one of your songs like that!' Andreas seem to puff between words, as if he is running, but Sakis knows it is just because he is unfit. 'Come up, Sakis! Come to Athens today. I can get you some great interviews and on the strength of this, we can go to New York, when, the day after? Also, I have a lead in Canada. You know, I think we can travel the world on this!'

There's a wilted lettuce leaf on the window ledge that Jules must have left, and Sakis gives it to the tortoise.

'Sakis, you there?' Andreas shouts from the telephone as Sakis attends the tortoise. 'What do you say? We can be in New York by the end of the week. Sakis? Sakis, are you listening?'

The tortoise is munching, a rhythmical sound, tapping out the time, and the birds sing another melody, this one a love song. With it, held high above the melody line, a bell rings, a high metallic chime. It is perfect. The pitch becomes more intense and he wakes from his daydream to see Abby tapping on the cottage's metal gate. Andreas is still talking in his ear.

'One minute, Andreas. I have something important I need to attend to…' And the phone is pocketed and forgotten.

Opening the gate, he invites her with no words and they stroll through the dried grass and into the dappled shade of the orange tree, his smile lighting up his eyes.

If you want updates from the Greek village between books why not subscribe to the free monthly newsletter for news and announcements.

Please visit http://www.saraalexi.com and click Newsletter.

Good reviews will help others find A Song Amongst the Orange Trees. If you enjoyed the book, please be kind and leave a review on Amazon.

Sincerely,

Sara Alexi

About Sara Alexi

Sara Alexi divides her time between England and a small village in Greece. She is working on her next novel in the Greek Village Series, to be released soon!

Sara Alexi is always delighted to receive emails from readers, and welcomes new friends on Facebook.

Email: saraalexi@me.com
Facebook:
        http://facebook.com/authorsaraalexi

Also by Sara Alexi

The Illegal Gardener
Black Butterflies
The Explosive Nature of Friendship
The Gypsy's Dream
The Art of Becoming Homeless
In the Shade of the Monkey Puzzle Tree
A Handful of Pebbles
The Unquiet Mind
Watching the Wind Blow
The Reluctant Baker
The English Lesson
The Priest's Well
The Stolen Book